LOVE UNDER RENOVATION

CLARA SINCLAIR

Love Under Renovation

Copyright © 2026 JWJ Hope

First Edition: February, 2026

ISBN: 9781067144609 (paperback)
ISBN: 9781067144616 (eBook)

Published by Hope Publishing, Auckland, New Zealand

For Claire, Karl, Genevieve, and Lachlan

CONTENTS

An Unexpected Opportunity   1

The Six A.M. Wake Up Call   14

The Willow Creek Welcome   29

The Wall   46

The Little Tin Box   57

The Storm and the Spark   66

One Step Forward...Two Steps Back   80

Roadtrip   94

The Grain and the Ghost   106

The Foundation of Doubt   116

Willow Creek Waltz   128

The Rhythm of the Hearth   146

An Unwanted Guest   155

The Blueprint of a Life   165

A Permanent Foundation   179

The Final Inspection   192

An Unexpected Opportunity

The email arrived when Ava Gardiner was hunched over her CAD workstation, squinting at elevation drawings for a minimalist Mc-Mansion in Westchester that her boss had promised the client by morning. It was 11:47pm. Her fourth coffee had gone cold an hour ago and had now formed a skin of milk fat and dust particles, and her neck graunched like someone had replaced her vertebrae with rusty hinges. She stretched, feeling her muscles complain from the atrophy, and glanced at the screen. The subject line read: "Estate of Beatrice Gardiner - Action Required."

Ava almost deleted it, her finger hovering over the track pad. She got fifty spam emails a day promising inheritances from Nigerian princes, cryptocurrencies from dead billionaires, and timeshares in properties from benevolent long lost relatives that didn't exist. But something made her pause.

Beatrice. Great Aunt Bea?

She clicked.

Twenty minutes later, she stood at her apartment window, staring out at the sliver of Chicago skyline visible from her small studio apartment, her phone pressed to her ear.

"This better be an emergency," her best friend Maya answered, voice thick with sleep. "Or proof of alien life. Those are the only acceptable reasons to call at midnight."

"You know my Great Aunt Bea who died?"

Silence. Then: "The one who sent you that taxidermied squirrel for Christmas?"

"She sent me a lot of weird things." Ava pressed her forehead against the cool glass. "Apparently she also left me a house."

"A house? Like, an actual house?" Maya was awake now.

"A cottage. In someplace called Willow Creek, Oregon." Ava turned back to her laptop, scrolling through the lawyer's email again. "According to this, it's been in the family for years and she wanted me to have it."

A rustle of sheets as Maya sat up. "Amazing, you could sell it. Finally, trade up to a place where your bedroom and kitchen aren't the same room."

Ava laughed, but it came out hollow. Her first thought had been putting the money toward her mountain of debt as the timing was almost too perfect. So many small debts but in 45 days the bank would trigger the default on her personal loan if she couldn't make the balloon payment. At best she would have to refinance again and take on even more crushing interest hikes. At worst she'd be destitute. Knocking off bills with money from Aunt Bea's house would free her up immensely. Things would be different if she'd got that promotion to Creative Director instead of Derek. Derek, who spent half his time playing ping-pong in the break room while she worked non-stop. Her savings account was laughable. A house, even a small one in the middle of nowhere, could solve everything.

"There's a catch," Ava said.

"Of course there is. It's a haunted cottage, isn't it? Tell me it's not haunted, ooh, actually tell me it is, it might raise the value!"

"The will stipulates that I have to stay there for thirty days before I can sell it. And according to the lawyer, the place needs work. Like, serious work. If I can't fix it up enough to get a decent price..." She trailed off, doing the math again in her head. The lawyer had been vague about the cottage's condition, which probably meant it was bad. But then again, even a modest sale price would be enough to put a serious dent in her debts. She'd need a bridging loan or line of credit for the renovation costs, but the cottage could secure that, and what's another loan at this point? Just add it to the pile. Thirty days to fix it up, a quick sale. The balloon payment would be doable, but tight...

"So you fix it up and sell it. You're an architect, Ava. You literally design buildings for a living," insisted Maya.

"I make pretty drawings of buildings. I haven't picked up a hammer since that disastrous IKEA bookshelf incident of 2019."

"We don't talk about the bookshelf incident." Maya paused. "How much time can you take off work?"

Ava glanced at her desk, the half-finished drawings, her calendar filled with meetings color-coded by level of soul-crushing tedium. She thought about her boss, Martin, who had looked right through her during the last staff meeting. Who had smiled sympathetically when he told her the promotion was going to Derek. It would serve him right if some of these projects faltered...

"I have three weeks of vacation saved up," she said slowly. "And if I add the week of sick days I never used and call it my bereavement leave...I can... Yeah, I can get to thirty days."

"You're actually considering this," Maya said approvingly.

Was she? Ava looked around her apartment, 350 square feet of beige walls and furniture she was still paying for, windows that mainly looked out at brick walls unless you got the angle just right, a kitchen so small she couldn't open the oven and refrigerator at the same time. She'd lived here for six years. Six years of telling herself it was temporary, that she was building toward something. This might be her one and only shot.

"I need that money, Maya. And it's just thirty days. I go out there, I fix up some charming cottage, I sell it, I come back and actually get my life together." She tried to sound confident. "How hard can it be?"

Maya was quiet for a moment but Ava knew she was making a face halfway between laughing and aghast. "You're going to hate every second of this, aren't you?" Maya finally said.

"Probably," Ava admitted. "But I'm good at doing things I hate. It's basically my entire life philosophy at this point."

"Wow. That's the saddest thing you've said all year, and you once told me you managed to kill a cactus."

"Hey, that wasn't my fault. It was clearly a very difficult plant to look after."

Maya laughed. "They're a plant that thrives on neglect, Ava!"

Ava gave a little laugh too. "I'll call Martin in the morning. Email the lawyer. I can probably be out there by the weekend."

"And if the cottage is a complete disaster?" Maya asked.

Ava stood up straight, staring out the window with more conviction than she could actually muster. "Then I'll have a complete disaster for thirty days, and then I'll never have to think about Willow Creek, Oregon ever again."

Ava had to remove the phone from her ear quickly to save her hearing from Maya's squeal of delight.

Two days later, Ava was on a flight to Portland which was delayed by three hours. She took it as an omen. She spent the time drafting yet another email to Martin with details of what needed to be done while she was gone. She rewrote it seven times before sending, each version a little less apologetic than the last. Overlooked for promotion but apparently too important to allow time to deal with her dead aunt's bequest, Martin's attitude didn't make Ava feel any less taken for granted. His response came through as she was boarding: "We'll discuss options when you return." Not "have a good trip." Not "hope it goes well." Just corporate-speak for "you're probably fired."

Ava shoved her phone in her bag and tried not to think about it. *Thirty days, get some money. Fix your life. Good times.*

The rental car was white and aggressively compact, the kind of vehicle that seemed designed to make her feel like she was playing pretend at being an adult. It would have been perfect for her usual haunts on busy Chicago streets, but Willow Creek had the ring of four wheel drive territory. Sadly, it was all the company had. She programmed Willow Creek into the GPS and started driving in a roughly easterly direction towards the Mt Hood National Forest, watching as urban Portland gave way to rugged countryside. City buildings became sprawling nursery lands, where Maples and Douglas Fir saplings sat in their thousands in ordered rows. Beyond the nurseries the order broke down and wild country set in. The saplings became giant Douglas Firs that were, in Ava's mind, as big as Chicago skyscrapers. Ava had grown up in suburbs, lived her adult life in cities. Mountains and forests were things she saw in photographs, preferably from the safety of sea level. Here, the suburbs were a distant memory, the only sign of civilization were rusted roof barns and tiny wood-sided houses. The air started to smell cold, a mix of damp earth, decaying pine needles, and imminent rain.

The drive gave her just enough time to spiral. Growing up, she never visited Aunt Bea, though Aunt Bea visited her and the family once or twice a year. The two of them had got on like a house on fire. Beatrice seemed to enjoy Ava's fiery spirit and curiosity, Ava enjoyed the endless stories and relaxed way of being that Beatrice had compared to her very strict and demanding parents. It had been a while since the last visit, Ava was always so busy these recent years. Now it was too late. A cold leaden weight of regret settled in her stomach, and with it came a flood of doubt. What if the cottage was worse than she thought? What if it was structurally unsound? What if there were raccoons? She hated raccoons. What if, what if...

Then, almost without warning, Willow Creek emerged from the forest like a secret being whispered into existence. A cluster of brick buildings nestled where the foothills met the flat. In the distance behind the town, Mount Hood rose like a benevolent guardian, its snow-capped peak catching the afternoon light and turning it to gold. The sight made something catch in Ava's throat. A hand-painted wooden sign proclaimed "Welcome to Willow Creek - Est. 1888 - Population 2,247," flanked by flower boxes overflowing with late-season petunias. Someone had been tending those flowers with devotion. The blooms were lush and cheerful, nodding in the breeze like a committee of grandmothers offering approval.

Ava slowed without deciding to, her foot easing off the gas as if the town itself was asking her to take her time. Main Street unfolded like a storybook illustration brought to life. Six blocks of brick storefronts lined both sides, hand-laid, slightly irregular, the mortar softened by age into something that looked almost organic. False-fronted buildings from the town's Wild West origins stood shoulder-to-shoulder with Arts and Crafts bungalows and Victorian flourishes. Nothing matched, yet everything belonged. At the heart stood a white church steeple, rising above the other buildings like an exclamation point. American flags were everywhere, fluttering from lamp posts and porch railings with earnest patriotism that felt almost innocent.

'Mama's Diner' sat beneath a cherry-red awning. Through wide picture windows, Ava saw checkered tablecloths and people bent over plates of food. The place radiated warmth, the kind of establishment where waitresses probably knew your order and called everyone "honey."

The 'Dust Jacket' a few doors down was a bookstore from the looks of it, occupying what had once been a house, its front porch converted into a reading nook with rocking chairs. A hand-painted sign announced poetry readings on Thursday nights. An orange tabby cat snoozed in the window display, surrounded by piles of books.

The town square opened on her left. A pocket park shaded by enormous oaks. Their canopy created a cathedral of green and dappled light playing off of a white Victorian gazebo with gingerbread trim. A farmers market was wrapping up, vendors packing the last of their produce. This was the kind of place that definitely had harvest festivals and town square concerts where everyone knew all the words. Where neighbors didn't just know each other's names, they knew each other's histories, heartbreaks, and hopes. The realization should have tightened like a noose. Instead, her chest loosened, making room for the strange, budding hope that belonging might actually be possible here.

The thought of that terrified her and she pushed it away. Having people know that much about you was an awful thought for a girl still mentally clad in city armor. This town was aggressively quaint. Offensively charming. Everything Ava had spent her adult life avoiding, slow, small, and impossibly earnest. There would be no caramel macchiatos here, no late-night takeout, no anonymity. Just this warm blanket of small-town life, wrapping around you whether you wanted it or not. The city-bred impulse to scoff at such provincial simplicity withered before it could take root. As the town stood still, something buried deep in her foundation began to shift and unfurl, anchoring her to this soil with the terrifying weight of a homecoming she hadn't authorized.

Ava shook the feeling off and doubled her resolve. *Thirty days. Just thirty days* her inner voice said.

The GPS directed her onto a side street that turned into a gravel road. Trees pressed in on both sides, their branches creating a canopy that blocked out most of the afternoon sun. Just when she was convinced she'd made a wrong turn, the path opened up to reveal a beautiful clearing. The titular creek went meandering off to her right somewhere, large weeping willows dipping their boughs into it along the bank. There were several cottages dotted around, all surrounded by beautiful gardens and picket fences.

And there it was.

Her cottage sat in a clearing surrounded by wildflowers and weeds in approximately equal measure. It was small, two floors, maybe eight hundred square feet, with faded yellow siding, white shutters hanging at unfortunate angles, and a front porch that sagged like a sigh. The roof looked like it had moss growing on it, at least one of the windows was cracked, and the garden was less of a garden and more of a warning about what happened when nature reclaimed its territory.

It was a disaster.

It was perfect.

It was going to take a lot more than thirty days!

The panic set in again and Ava sat in the rental car, hands still on the wheel, fighting that despair settling in her chest. She could fix this. She had to fix this. She'd figure it out, make a plan, find contractors, throw what little money she had at the problem until it looked presentable enough to sell. *Breathe slow, breathe deep...* She was still trying to convince herself of this plan when she heard the knock on her car window.

Ava jumped, hand flying to her chest, and turned to see a man standing beside her car. Tall, broad-shouldered, square set and rugged wearing a flannel shirt with the sleeves rolled up and an expression that suggested she was the most inconvenient thing that had happened to him all week. He made a rolling motion with his hand. She lowered the window.

"You're going to want to move your car," he said without preamble. His voice was deep, and rough around the edges. "You're blocking the road."

Ava was shaken from away from her inner thoughts and tried to reconnect with reality. "Sorry?" she said.

His neck seemed to flex. "The road. I need to use it to get my truck out. And you're blocking it."

The man clearly wore his grumpiness like armor, a carefully cultivated shield of scowls and terse replies that kept strangers at a safe distance. *I thought small town folk were meant to be nice,* she thought.

"Right. Sorry." She wasn't sorry. She was tired and stressed and frazzled now because this man was glaring at her like she'd personally ruined his day. "Are you always this friendly, or is this special service for newcomers?" she asked.

Good way to make friends with the neighbours. It's a good thing you're not staying long.

Something flickered across his face, surprise, maybe, or irritation. "Move the car. Please." The 'please' sounded like it cost him something, it was short and terse and he didn't want to part with it.

Ava put the car in reverse, backed up about twenty feet, and parked on what might have been the edge of someone's lawn. It might have even been hers. When she got out, the man was still there, watching her with his arms crossed. Up close, her eye was drawn to his dark hair that needed a cut, green eyes that were probably attractive when they weren't narrowed in annoyance, and sawdust on his jeans. He looked like he'd stepped out of some rustic catalog selling an expensive fantasy of rural masculinity. Or a kids book about Paul Bunyan.

Ava put on her Chicago mental armor and lifted her chin. "Better?"

"You're the one who inherited Beatrice's place" he said, pointing at the cottage.

It wasn't a question, but she answered anyway. "Ava Gardiner. And you are?"

"Liam McGregor." He glanced at the cottage, then back at her, and something in his expression shifted, still not friendly, but maybe less actively hostile. "Beatrice was a good person. I'm sorry for your loss."

The unexpected kindness caught her off guard. "Thank you. I didn't know her very well, honestly. It had...been a while." She looked down, trying to hide her guilt.

"She talked about you. Sometimes." Liam shifted his weight, looking uncomfortable. "Said you were too smart to waste your life on things that didn't matter."

Ava blinked, the surprise telling on her face. "She said that?"

"She had opinions." The corner of his mouth twitched, almost like he might smile. He didn't. "You're planning to fix this placc up?"

"And sell it, yes. I have thirty days before I need to be back in Chicago, so I'm planning on a quick turnaround. Tackle the...worst of it..." She trailed off. From here it was hard to discern what wasn't 'the worst of it'. It was a pretty even field.

Now he did smile, but it wasn't comforting. "Good luck with that" he grunted.

"What's that supposed to mean?"

"It means this cottage isn't for flipping and making city profits. It needs roof work. Foundation work. Probably new plumbing, and definitely a new porch bcforc somconc falls through it and sues you." IIe ticked the items off on his fingers like he was reading a grocery list. "Thirty days isn't going to cut it."

Ava's anxiety crystallized into anger, "I didn't ask for your assessment," she snapped, with a little too much force. Mr Grumpy may have known Aunt Bea, but he didn't know her and what she could do, and she was already looking forward to never having to see him again. She just hoped he wasn't a neighbor.

"Nope. But you're going to need it. You rang ahead to Harper and Bayley?"

The Real Estate agents. Ava nodded.

"Well, Willow Creek doesn't have a large pool of contractors to call on, in fact there's exactly one who can do this kind of work on short notice." He paused, and she realized with growing horror what he was about to say.

Don't say it, don't say it.

"That's me."

Of course it was. Of course the only person who could help her was this grumpy, flannel-wearing mountain man who looked at her like she was a problem he didn't want to solve.

"I know Alice Harper pretty well, and she didn't want you to waste time spending a day ringing around and not getting anywhere. Might as well cut to the chase."

Ava took a breath. Internally she said words that Aunt Bea would not have approved of and fought back the sarcastic voice of failure stirring in her head. Thirty days. She could work with anyone for thirty days, right? Even someone who apparently communicated primarily through scowls and devastating property assessments.

She forced herself to smile.

"Fine," she said. "I guess I don't have time or the local knowledge to argue. How much?"

Liam named a figure that made her wince but was, annoyingly, probably fair given the circumstances.

"I can start tomorrow. But I'm going to need you to be around" he said. "This isn't the kind of job where I can just hand you a key at the end. I'll need your input. And, if you want to be done in thirty days, your help." He looked her up and down in a way that indicated he didn't expect much in the way of help.

Ava chose to ignore it. "I'll be here. It's not like I have anywhere else to be" she said.

Something crossed his face again, like he was trying not to immediately dismiss her and send her packing. But before she could actually identify it, he was turning away, heading toward a truck parked on the other side of the cottage. It was dark green, older, covered in a fine layer of dust that somehow made it look more authentic.

"McGregor," she called after him.

He stopped, looked back.

"Why are you helping me? You clearly don't want to."

For a long moment, he just looked at her, and Ava had the strange sensation of being truly seen for the first time in months. Not assessed or dismissed or overlooked, but actually noticed.

"I promised Beatrice I'd look after the place," he said finally. "Didn't realize that meant looking after you too."

Before she could decide if that was insulting or oddly sweet, he was in his truck and driving away, leaving her standing alone in front of a cottage that looked one strong breeze away from collapse, in a town she didn't want to be in.

Ava pulled out her phone and took a picture. She sent it to Maya with the caption: "I've made a huge mistake. And the builder hates me."

The response came immediately: "It's cute! Very murder-mystery-weekend-getaway."

"That's not reassuring."

"Is the builder hot?"

Ava looked at the dust trail from Liam's truck, disappearing into the trees.

"Irrelevant," she typed back.

"So yes. This is going to be amazing!!"

Ava pocketed her phone, grabbed her suitcase from the car, and walked up to the cottage. The key the lawyer had sent her got stuck in the lock, and she had to jiggle it for a full minute before the door finally opened with a groan that sounded almost human.

Inside, the cottage smelled like dust and old lavender and something else she couldn't quite identify. Maybe it was time standing still, or the smell of a thousand hours of baking having seeped into the wood. The larger furniture was covered in white sheets that made everything look like ghosts. Afternoon light filtered through the dirty windows, painting everything in gold. On the mantel sat a small taxidermied squirrel like the one her aunt had sent her for Christmas. It looked to be the twin of her own and the memory of it made her sad.

Her quick assessment started taking in everything wrong with the interior. The words "dated" and "potentially unsafe" came to mind in equal measure. Some of the fixtures and fitting were clearly not in working order, looking dated and run down. Ava supposed her aunt's final years didn't include a lot of maintenance and upkeep. To Ava's modern eye, parts might not have been up to scratch when they were new. Still, some of the interior molding and detail would be quite nice with a little TLC, so perhaps not all was lost. But this was going to take every penny she had and then some from the looks of it, and she didn't even know if this little town would carry the supplies needed to rescue this place. She was at the mercy of Liam McGregor on that front. It was absolutely not what she'd signed up for.

Ava set down her suitcase and looked around at what would be her home for the next thirty days. Nothing to do but make a start.

"Okay, Aunt Beatrice," she said to the empty room. "Let's see what you got me into."

She got out a large sheet of paper and a marker. She'd started to put together her timeline and schedule on the flight and now she was here and could see what she was dealing with, she could fill in some of the details. Outside, through the cracked window, birds were singing, wind moved through the pines and the willows, and somewhere in the distance, the sound of the creek, with its gentle and rhythmic tones she hadn't noticed before, played their tune. The pleasant noises kept her company while she worked, and when finished, miraculously fitting it all on one page, she stuck the schedule to the fridge with an Oregon magnet Aunt Bea had left. First job done.

Despite everything: her better judgment, the grumpy carpenter, the impossible timeline, and her entire life falling apart back in Chicago, Ava felt something small and stubborn unfold in her chest. Not quite hope, but maybe, possibly, the beginning of something like it.

She'd give it thirty days to find out.

The Six A.M. Wake Up Call

The sound of something being violently destroyed yanked Ava from sleep like a fire alarm. She bolted upright in bed, heart hammering, momentarily disoriented by the slanted ceiling and the unfamiliar smell of mothballs mixed with dried lavender.

What on earth was that? Where am I? Is the world ending?

The guest room. Aunt Bea's cottage. Right.

Another thunderous crash echoed from downstairs, followed by the unmistakable sound of splintering wood. She grabbed her phone from the nightstand then threw it down again when she saw it was 6:14 a.m.

"You have got to be kidding me," she muttered, throwing off the ancient quilt that had kept her alternating between too hot and too cold all night. The hardwood floor was ice against her bare feet. Her breath formed a faint vapour in front of her, evidence of the chilly start to the day. Apparently, Great Aunt Beatrice hadn't believed in central heating. Or insulation. Or any modern comfort invented after 1975.

She caught sight of herself in the tarnished mirror above the dresser and winced. Her hair had achieved a level of chaos that defied physics. There were pillow creases on her face, and were those actual bags under her eyes, or had the mirror's oxidation created unfortunate shadows?

Another crash shook the floorboards.

Ava pulled on her cashmere lounge set, soft gray, expensive, designed for lazy Sundays in climate-controlled apartments, not construction sites in the Oregon wilderness. Her suitcase sat open in the corner, her suede ankle boots from yesterday, now covered in mud and possibly ruined beyond repair, dumped unceremoniously alongside. She'd paid $300 for those boots and the thought of that didn't improve her mood. She was going to kill Liam McGregor, assuming he hadn't already demolished the entire cottage before she could get downstairs.

The scene that greeted her in the kitchen was like something from a home renovation show, if the show was directed by someone with a vendetta against structural stability. Liam stood in the middle of what had previously been a wall separating the kitchen from the hallway, sledgehammer in hand, surrounded by a cloud of plaster dust that caught the early morning light like snow. He'd already torn out a section roughly four feet wide, exposing old wiring that looked like it predated the Eisenhower Administration.

He was wearing a different flannel, clearly a uniform of sorts for him. This one was blue and gray, with the sleeves rolled up to reveal forearms that were frankly distracting. Ava didn't know there were muscles there that would ripple like that, but she didn't have the time or the patience to admire them further. There was dust in his hair. His work boots had left tracks across the worn linoleum. And he was humming. Actually humming, like destroying her inherited property at dawn was the highlight of his week.

"What," she said, focusing her outrage, her voice coming out higher than intended, "do you think you're doing?"

Liam turned, and had the audacity to look surprised to see her, but his Mr Grumpy persona was obviously still in full effect. "Working," he said sharply. "We agreed I'd start today."

"'Today' doesn't start at six in the morning!" Ava exclaimed.

"Does round here. Especially on a construction site." He set the sledgehammer against the wall with a gentleness that seemed at odds with what he'd been doing with it. "You want this done in thirty days. We don't have time to waste."

Ava pressed her fingers to her temples, trying to stave off the headache already forming behind her eyes. She hadn't even had coffee yet. She couldn't deal with this without coffee. She took a breath.

"Do you have coffee?" she asked, exercising the maximum amount of calm she could muster.

"Do I look like a coffee shop?" Liam retorted.

"Do you want me to answer that honestly?" Ava fired back.

Something flickered in his expression, this time Ava was pretty sure it was amusement as one side of his mouth twitched, but it was gone too quickly to be sure. He reached for a battered metal thermos sitting on what remained of the kitchen counter. "You're going to have to sort out your own supplies long term. But here," he said, pouring a stream of liquid so dark it was almost black into a chipped mug. He held it out to her. "Just this once."

The smell hit her the moment she took the mug: strong, bitter, the kind of coffee that could probably strip paint. It was perfect. Even just the aroma sent energy coursing through her brain and civility returned to Ava's thoughts. She held the mug like it was a lifeline, wrapping both hands around it even though it was too hot. The first sip burned her tongue and tasted like it had been brewed with contempt for weakness, but the caffeine hit her system like a blessing. "Thank you," she said, letting out a slow, satisfied breath.

Liam nodded with a small grunt, then went back to examining the wall he'd partially destroyed, apparently considering their conversation over.

Ava was trying to formulate a coherent thought about schedules and reasonable working hours when she heard a sound from the direction of the front door, a scrabbling of claws on hardwood, followed by the appearance of the shaggiest dog she'd ever seen. He was medium-sized, with wiry gray and white fur that stuck out in all directions, soulful brown eyes, and a tail that wagged with such enthusiasm his entire back half moved with it. He spotted Ava and made a beeline straight for her, nearly knocking the coffee from her hands in his eagerness to say hello.

"Barnaby, down," Liam said without really turning around. "And don't get close to her, she doesn't like mornings," he added.

Barnaby ignored this completely, instead sitting directly at Ava's feet and gazing up at her with an expression of absolute adoration. She bent down and gave the dog a big hug. "He doesn't listen to you, does he?" Ava said, unable to stop herself from smiling. His fur was surprisingly soft under all that chaos.

"He listens fine. He just doesn't care." Liam glanced back at them, and something in his expression softened when he saw Barnaby and Ava like long lost best friends. "He...he usually doesn't take to strangers that fast."

"I'm very likeable," Ava said, then reconsidered. "Actually, I'm moderately likeable. I think your dog might just have poor judgment."

"Possible." Liam picked up a pry bar from his tool belt. "He thinks squirrels are his mortal enemies and that the mailman is trying to steal the house, so his threat assessment is questionable at best."

It was the most Liam had said to her at once in a tone that wasn't angry or dismissive, and Ava found herself studying him in the strengthening daylight. There was dust on his cheekbone. His hands, when he gripped the pry bar, were scarred and callused in a way that suggested years of work. He moved around the destruction with the easy confidence of someone completely in his element. His eyes moved around the wall in front of him, taking in each nail, beam, or piece of plaster and like a master he knew where to apply pressure to remove the old and worn out cleanly, and what might be left alone and saved. She hated that she found it attractive.

"So," Ava said, stepping carefully around Barnaby to approach what remained of the wall. "You just decided to start demolition without consulting me?"

"You hired me to fix the house. This is fixing."

"This is destroying."

"Same thing. First few days." Liam wedged the pry bar under a piece of baseboard and pulled. It came away with a screech of nails, revealing more of the wall cavity. "You can't build something new without taking apart what's broken."

"Very philosophical. Did you workshop that, or does it come naturally?" She sipped her coffee.

He almost smiled, that twitch in the corner of his mouth again before he suppressed it. "You're mouthy for someone who doesn't know a stud from a joist."

"I'm an architect. I know exactly what a stud is" said Ava, matter of factly.

"Knowing how to draw it and knowing how to work with it are different." He set down the pry bar and pulled out his phone, swiping to a photo. "This is what I found when I got here this morning."

He held it out to her. The photo showed the space behind the wall he'd demolished, and the wiring there looked like something from a museum exhibit on electrical fires waiting to happen.

"Ugh. That's a fire hazard," Ava said quietly.

"That's a miracle this place hasn't burned down already." Liam pocketed his phone. "The main board needs to be replaced, and we ought to do all the sockets. Which means opening up walls. Which is why I started early. We're already behind, and we haven't even begun."

To stave off a pang of anxiety, Ava took another sip of the terrible, wonderful coffee and forced herself to think practically. He was right. She hated that he was right, but the evidence was literally hanging out of the wall in front of her. Her practical brain kicked into gear: schedule impact? New materials required? We need a plan and action points.

"Okay," she said. "Fine. Demo the walls. But we need a plan. A real plan, not just you showing up at dawn to destroy things."

"I have a plan."

"Does it involve permits? Inspections? A timeline?"

"It involves fixing the house so it doesn't kill the next person who lives here."

"That's not a plan. That's a philosophy." She went to the fridge to get the schedule.

Liam turned to face her fully, looking like he was a volcano of annoyance on the verge of exploding. Ava became acutely aware of how small the kitchen was, or maybe it was that he seemed to take up more space than he should, his presence somehow filling the room. This was his happy place where he had immense skill and knowledge. He owned the chaos around him and Ava was acutely aware she was out of her element. She was also very aware that he smelled like sawdust and coffee and something else, soap, maybe, or just the clean scent of early morning air.

"You want a plan?" he said. "Here's the plan. We gut the kitchen and the bathroom. Replace the electrical box and the sockets. Shore up the foundation where it's settling. Patch the roof. Replace the broken windows. Refinish the floors. Might need to update the heating system. Then, if we have time, we make the rest pretty."

Ahh, now the conversation was moving into Ava's happy place: design and appeal.

"If we have time?" Ava set her coffee down on the counter with more force than necessary. "Pretty is the whole point. I need this house to sell. That means it needs to look good, not just function."

"It needs to do both," he growled.

"I'm aware of that. I'm also aware that buyers don't care about new wiring if the kitchen looks like it hasn't been updated since the 70's. A buyer, any buyer, wants to feel comfortable and see themselves in the space, and an empty house with good joists won't cut it." She finished a little more curtly than perhaps necessary.

They stared at each other across the demolished wall, and Ava could feel her pulse thrumming in her throat. This was exactly what she'd been afraid of, being stuck in the middle of nowhere with someone who didn't understand that she had a deadline, she had debts, and that she didn't have the luxury of noble restoration projects. Barnaby whined softly, looking between them like he was watching a tennis match.

Liam exhaled slowly. "What do you want? Exactly."

Ava pulled out her tablet from where she'd left it on the counter last night. She'd spent hours working on a renovation plan, mapping out finishes, creating mood boards, calculating costs.

"I want open-concept," she said, pulling up her design. "Kitchen, dining, and living room as one flow. Light wood floors, white subway tile backsplash, granite or marble countertops. Modern farmhouse aesthetic. It's what sells right now. Clean lines, neutral palette, Instagram-ready."

She turned the tablet to show him her rendering. It was good work, if she said so herself. The kind of space that would photograph beautifully for a listing, and could be snapped up by an investor within a matter of days.

Liam looked at it for a long moment. She thought she heard his teeth grinding. Then he looked at the cottage around them, the original built-in hutch with its wavy glass doors, the deep windowsills, the archway between rooms with its carved trim.

"You want to gut it," he sneered.

"I want to update it" Ava said, with a bit more sweetness in her voice than she'd shown so far this morning.

"There's a pantry behind that wall," he pointed. "It's original to the house. Custom shelving, built-in flour bin, even the old hooks where Beatrice hung her herbs to dry."

"It's a pantry. I can buy one from IKEA."

"It's not the same."

"It's functionally identical."

"It's not about function." Liam's voice had gone quiet in a way that was more dangerous than if he'd yelled. "This house has a soul. It has history. Beatrice lived here for sixty years. She chose you to inherit it. And you want to turn it into something you'd find in a catalog and flick it off?" He spat the last few words like they were a terrible insult.

The words hit harder than Ava expected. Her cheeks flushed red hot, and something uncomfortably close to shame stirred in her chest. With great control, she kept her voice level. It took a lot of effort. "I appreciate that Aunt Bea thought of me, but I can't afford sentiment. I need to sell this house. To do that, it needs to appeal to buyers. Buyers want modern. They want clean. They don't care about original pantries or history, they care about granite countertops and open floor plans."

"Then maybe you're selling to the wrong buyers." Liam said curtly.

"I'm selling to whoever will give me enough money to pay my debts and go back to my actual life!"

The words came out louder than she'd intended, echoing in the small space. Barnaby's ears drooped and he whined slightly. *So much for self control* thought Ava, who hadn't intended to share her private details or needs with the contractor. She stood there silently, unsure where to go next.

Liam was quiet too, his jaw working like he was chewing on something he didn't want to say. He was first to speak, and when he finally spoke his voice was carefully neutral like he was holding back a lot of what he actually wanted to say. "Okay," he said. "Here's what we're going to do. I'll handle the bones, the structure, the systems, the things that actually matter. You handle the...finishes. The paint colors, the fixtures, whatever Pinterest told you to buy. But I'm keeping the pantry."

"!" said Ava.

"Non-negotiable. And the built-in hutch in the dining room. And the picture rail molding." He ticked them off on his fingers like she had yesterday. "Everything else, we can discuss."

"It's my house!"

"It's my work. In my town. And I know what this house needs and what this town can deliver in thirty days. More than you do."

She took a deep breath. He had her there. Except for the molding (which, she had to admit, was quite nice) it wasn't what Ava wanted. But looking at the set of his shoulders, the firmness in his voice, she knew it was the best deal she was going to get from him. And she needed him. She needed his skills and his knowledge of the area. There wasn't time to find another contractor, even if one existed in this tiny town, and there was no point if the local Mom and Pop Hardware store was the only place to get anything. She didn't know what supplies or scale of renovation the town could help with in thirty days. And he sure looked like he knew what he was doing.

"Fine," she said stubbornly so as not to lose all control of the conversation. "But I'm not promising to like it."

"I'm not promising to care if you do."

They glared at each other, cold and steely. Barnaby looked between them hopefully, like he thought they might start playing fetch at any moment. He nudged his nose against Ava's leg and it successfully broke the silence between them.

"So what now?" Ava asked finally.

Liam reached down and picked up a pry bar from his tool belt. He held it out to her.

"You work."

Ava looked at the tool like it might bite her. "What?"

"You want this done in thirty days? You're not an executive giving orders, you're labor, remember? I can't do this alone, and I can't afford to hire a crew for what you're paying me."

"But I don't know how to use...that," Ava said.

"I'll teach you." He waited, the pry bar still extended. "Unless you'd rather go back to bed and let me handle everything while you check your email?"

It was a challenge. They both knew it. Ava set down her coffee and took the pry bar. It was heavier than it looked, the metal cool in her palm. "Fine. Where do I start?"

A brief look of respect passed through Liam's eyes, or perhaps it was surprise that she had agreed. He gave a slight nod, which Ava suspected counted as 'high praise' from him. "Baseboard. Start in the corner, work your way along. Wedge the flat end under the board, lever it away from the wall. Try not to damage the wood if you can help it."

He moved to stand beside her, close enough to see the stubble on his jaw, the small scar above his left eyebrow, and the way his eyes were actually more hazel than green this close up in the morning light. He reached around her to adjust the bar against the wall. "Like this," he said, his voice low and close to her ear. "Gentle pressure first. Find where it's nailed. Then quick, firm leverage."

Ava focused on the baseboard and not at all on the way his breath stirred her hair or the fact that he smelled like pine and coffee.

"Got it?" he asked.

"Got it," she managed. She wedged the pry bar under the baseboard and pulled.

Her hands flew off the bar, which clattered to the floor, and she almost hit him in the face as they flailed backwards.

"You have to grip it!" he barked with an annoyed, and yet somewhat amused tone.

"I *was* gripping it. It slipped." A red heat of embarrassment started to rise from her chest and creep up her neck. This was worse than the IKEA bookshelf. She wasn't going to fail at the first hurdle though and she replaced the bar for a second go. "Like this?" she asked.

He adjusted the bar on the baseboard again slightly. "Yes. Now don't forget…"

"Grip it, yes I know!" she snapped. She doubled her grip and pulled. Nothing happened, but since she didn't fall or hit him with the pry bar, it was definitely an improvement. She adjusted her position and tried again, putting more force behind it. The baseboard screeched in protest but started to come away from the wall. Triumph surged through her… right before her hands slipped again and she stumbled backward.

This time, Liam caught her elbow, steadying her. "It's not a race."

His grip was strong, safe and secure. His large powerful hands were, somehow, also gentle and reassuring.

"You said we don't have time to waste," she said, standing up and shaking off thoughts of large hands.

"We don't have time to waste at the emergency room either," he said shortly, but there was something almost like approval in his voice.

Ava repositioned to try again, more carefully this time. He made a minor adjustment to the position of the bar, before taking a small step to his right, away from any potential flying bar or flailing arms. She glanced at him accusatorily.

He looked back with raised eyebrows as if to say "what?" but sensibly stayed silent.

She gripped the pry bar as tight as she could and pulled. The baseboard came away inch by inch, nails shrieking as they pulled free. When it finally came loose completely, she felt ridiculously proud of herself.

"Good," Liam said. "Now do it again. All along this wall."

For the next hour, they worked in a silence broken only by the sounds of demolition: wood splintering, nails squealing, the occasional muttered curse when something didn't come free easily. Despite her best efforts, her amateur skill with a pry bar left dents and damage along the wooden wall, but at least the baseboard was clear. Barnaby supervised from a safe distance, occasionally sighing like he found the whole endeavor tedious. Ava's arms started to ache. Then burn. Her cashmere lounge set was covered in dust and she mentally added it to the shoes upstairs as part of a growing list of possessions that this cottage had ruined so far. She was pretty sure she had a blister forming on her palm. But somehow, impossibly, she was almost enjoying herself.

There was something satisfying about the physical work, about seeing tangible progress and an improvement in her skills with every passing minute. The dents and damage to the wall were not a lot less frequent for example. In her regular job, results were nebulous: approvals took weeks, designs were submitted that might never get built, meetings achieved nothing. This was immediate. She pulled. The board came free. She moved on to the next one. She was prying up the last section when Liam called out, "Stop."

Ava froze, the pry bar still wedged under the baseboard. "What?"

He was crouched a few feet away, examining something in the wall cavity he'd exposed. His expression somewhere between puzzled and concerned. "Come look at this."

Ava set down the pry bar and moved to where he was kneeling. She had to get close to see what he was pointing at and took in that smell of sawdust, pine, and soap again. He pointed to a gap between the original plaster and the newer drywall someone had installed over it. There, tucked into the narrow space, was what looked like a small metal box. It was roughly the size of a shoebox, made of tin that had oxidized to a mottled gray-green. Through the dust, Ava could just make out flowers, or vines painted on the lid. Before she could take in the detail or think to pick it up, a sudden hiss cut her off. They both looked up at the ceiling.

An old copper pipe ran along the exposed joist. The hiss became a drip, then a stream, then a small jet of rusty water pouring directly onto the floor where they'd been working. "Damn it," Liam barked, already moving. He grabbed a bucket from his supplies and positioned it under the leak, then reached up to trace the pipe. "This whole section is corroded. I must have bumped it when I was working on the wall."

The water was spreading across the floor, soaking into the edges of their demolition site and into the floorboards. Barnaby retreated to higher ground with a disgruntled bark. Ava looked from the growing puddle to Liam's grim expression. "Is this going to delay us?" she asked.

Liam resisted the urge for a sarcastic response, and tested the pipe carefully with his hand. Another spray of water rewarded his efforts. "It's the main supply line to the kitchen. I'll need to shut off the water to the house, cut out this section, and replace it. Four hours, minimum. Longer if the damage is worse than it looks."

Any thought of the box disappeared from Ava's head. "Four hours we don't have," she whined.

"Four hours, or we don't have water." He looked at her, and she saw the frustration there that matched her own. "This is what I meant. The house is full of problems we can't see until we start tearing into it. We can stick to your schedule or we can do this right. We can't do both."

Ava wanted to argue. Wanted to insist that they could do both, that with enough planning and effort they could meet her deadline without compromise if he wasn't so pig-headed. But the water was still pouring into the bucket, the exposed walls were revealing more problems than solutions, and her arms hurt from an hour of manual labor. Liam started for his truck, presumably to get supplies. "There's a shut-off valve in the crawlspace. I need you to turn it clockwise until it won't turn anymore."

"Where's the crawlspace?"

"Trap door, in the pantry. You'll need a flashlight." He paused at the front door. "And watch your head." Then he was gone, before reappearing again to add "and if you see any eyes down there, they are probably just raccoons. Probably." Then he disappeared, leaving her alone with a flooded floor and instructions to descend into what was probably a spider-infested horror show under the house. Barnaby gave an encouraging bark from the far side of the kitchen, with an expression that suggested he, too, thought this was a terrible idea but was willing to provide moral support.

"Your owner is insane," Ava told him. Barnaby wagged his tail.

Ava found a flashlight in one of the toolboxes, opened the door to the pantry and found the small square hatchway that was the crawlspace access. She lifted it with some effort, and looked down into darkness that smelled like damp earth, ancient dust, and possibly raccoons. Evil raccoons. She didn't like small spaces. Or crowds. Or large social gatherings... but things that crawl, or could jump out at her topped the list. She could feel her heart start to pound and the tell tale restriction of a panic attack in her throat at the thought of being trapped below the house.

She took several big deep breaths and tried to get her thoughts under control. First, she thought about her apartment in Chicago. Her climate-controlled, well-lit, structurally sound though very, very small apartment with its reliable plumbing and distinct lack of disasters waiting to be discovered. Then she thought about her loan, the upcoming default if she didn't succeed here. And her soul crushing job... But then she thought about Liam saying she was labor now, not an executive, and the small part of her that had been thrilled at proving she could do the work. Her breathing slowed and her intrusive thoughts were beaten back into the recesses of her mind. "Okay, Aunt Bea," she muttered, gathering up her courage and control. "This better be worth it."

She took a step down and heard her feet touch water. "You've got to be kidding," she said with a mix of rage and exasperation. Descending from the pantry into the crawlspace was like sliding into a shallow, wooden grave. The ceiling, which was actually the underside of the kitchen floorjoists, hovered a mere twenty-four inches above the dirt, forcing Ava onto her belly in a space that smelled of ancient dust and the sharp, metallic tang of damp earth. Every time she moved, the rough-sawn timber scraped against her shoulder blades, a constant, claustrophobic reminder of the thousands of pounds of Victorian architecture resting just inches above her spine. The beam of her flashlight was swallowed by the oppressive darkness, catching only the glistening silver of spiderwebs and the occasional rib-cage of a floor support. As she dragged herself forward over a crinkling plastic vapor barrier, the air grew thick and stagnant, vibrating with the muffled, heavy *thrum* of the water falling down onto the kitchen floor and then again down onto the plastic sheet, making her feel as though she were being buried alive beneath the very house she was trying to save.

This outfit was definitely not going to be salvageable.

The flashlight beam trembled in her hand, or maybe that was just her shaking, revealing cobwebs thick as curtains and dark corners where anything could be lurking. Raccoons. Spiders. God knew what else called this place home. There were pipes running along the joists and Ava followed them with her eyes towards the front of the house to a valve lurking in the darkness. She crawled along on her belly, trying desperately to avoid hitting her head, or worse, collecting any spiders (or raccoons) clinging to the floorboards above her. The initial few feet were tricky, as the water not only made her wet and uncomfortable, it added a degree of slipperiness that made manoeuvring extra difficult, but once past the worst of the flooding, it became easier.

Following the pipes, she made it to the shut-off valve, crusted with rust and years of neglect. Ava refused to shine the torch around for fear of finding something looking back, and focussed with steely determination on getting the valve to move. Holding the torch in her mouth, she gripped the valve with both hands and pushed.

Nothing.

She braced her feet and tried again, muscles screaming, palms slipping on the corroded metal. This was the biggest challenge the house had sent her so far and she was determined not to be beaten.

Come on, come on, come on.

With a screech that echoed through the darkness, the valve finally gave. She cranked it clockwise until it wouldn't turn anymore, her heart hammering against her ribs.

Silence. The dripping upstairs stopped.

Ava lay in the dim crawlspace, breathing hard. Pride started to swell in her chest, a little at first but then blooming like an unfolding flower. She'd done it. City girl Ava Gardiner, who paid people to change her lightbulbs, had just saved her kitchen from flooding. She was elated!

Above her, Liam's boots crossed the floor. "Ava? You good?" he called out.

Elation gave way to realization she was still in an Evil Raccoon and spider filled horror dungeon and she made for the crawlspace door as close to double pace as she could manage in the tight, claustrophobic space. She finally emerged on shaking legs, filthy, and sopping wet in places. But she was back in the light and relative cleanliness of the kitchen, with cobwebs in her hair and triumph in her smile. Challenge one complete. Thirty days. She could survive thirty days of anything.

But she wasn't doing that again!

The Willow Creek Welcome

The gravel crunched beneath Ava's designer boots as she stared at her rental car, gleaming incongruously against the weathered backdrop of Aunt Beatrice's cottage. Liam stood in the doorway, one hand on his hip, the other holding his coffee cup, that infuriating half-smirk playing at the corners of his mouth.

"You want me to drive myself?" she asked, waving around the list of supplies Liam had given her and trying to keep the disbelief from her voice. Unsuccessfully.

"Unless you can carry it all on your back." He gestured toward her car with his coffee mug. "Town's ten minutes down the road. Can't miss it. It's the only thing between here and the county line."

"You could just give me a ride in your truck," she suggested.

"Could." He took a slow sip of coffee, those hazel eyes never leaving hers. "But then you wouldn't get the full Willow Creek experience. Plus I have work to do."

Ava had barely slept. Yesterday's adventure of the kitchen pipe had left her feeling quite buoyant, to actually have faced a disaster and come through, but while the physical work had left her physically exhausted, she couldn't help but get occasional flashes in her mind of strong hands, and aromas of coffee, sawdust, and soap. They had kept her awake. If it hadn't been for more of Liam's nuclear coffee she'd be dead on her feet. But now he was back to being cryptic and impossible and any nice thoughts were rapidly being overcome by her annoyance of him again. *Men are infuriating,* she thought.

"Fine." She snatched her keys from her pocket with more force than necessary. "I'll go myself."

"Ava." Something in his voice made her pause. When she turned back, his expression had softened almost imperceptibly. "Stay on the main road. The gravel can be difficult. If you're not used to it."

The concern in his warning sent an unwanted flutter through her chest. She nodded curtly and climbed into her car before she could do something ridiculous like thank him for caring.

The road to Willow Creek wound through a landscape that seemed determined to break through Ava's defenses. Weeping willows, ordered, well measured and lined up along the water way that gave the town its name, their reflections shimmering in water so clear the smooth stones on the bottom were plainly visible. She'd been so keen to find the cottage she hadn't noticed the beauty all around her on her previous drive. Morning mist still clung to the hollows between hills, and the early light turned everything golden and impossibly soft.

Don't get attached, she reminded herself, gripping the steering wheel tighter. *Thirty days and you'll be back in Chicago where you belong.*

But even as she thought it, she couldn't quite summon the usual conviction. Chicago meant her office, her efficient routines, her carefully constructed walls that kept everything, and everyone, at a safe distance. But Chicago meant going days without a real conversation, eating takeout alone at her desk, falling asleep to the sound of sirens instead of creek water. Chicago meant never having someone look at her the way Liam had yesterday, like he could see straight through her armor to something she'd forgotten was there.

Her phone buzzed. Another text from Martin: *Board meeting moved to Thursday. Need your projections ASAP.* The real world, reminding her that she had responsibilities, a career, a life that didn't involve muddy boots and infuriating contractors with eyes like a gathering storm and who won't just do what you tell them.

She was so lost in thought that she almost missed the turn into town. Willow Creek appeared suddenly around a bend, that cluster of brick buildings huddled together like they were sharing secrets. She passed a post office, a barbershop with an actual striped pole, a pharmacy with a hand-painted sign, and then her stomach growled, making the decision about her first stop for her.

Mama's Diner, the one with the red awning she noticed on the way into town the other day, sat on the corner like it had been there since the dawn of time. A red neon sign proclaiming "HOME COOKING" in letters that had probably been bright once, but was now a more mellow suggestion much more in keeping with the relaxed nature of the town, and what home cooking should be. The smell of coffee and bacon was wafting into the street from an open window, inviting anyone nearby to be dragged in by the nostrils like in old cartoons.

The moment she pushed through the door, every head in the place turned. The diner wasn't full, but the eyes on Ava filled up the world. The scrape of forks against plates stopped and conversations died mid-sentence. Ava couldn't help but think how it was like an old Western movie where the man in the black hat enters through the saloon door and the piano stops. In keeping with that, somewhere in the back, a radio played an old country song, though it might as well have been a funeral dirge for all the sudden attention had the air and gravity of a burial.

Stranger in a small town, she thought.

Ava's corporate instincts kicked in. Smile. Make eye contact. Project confidence. She'd walked into hostile boardrooms and come out victorious. She could handle a small-town diner. Before she could re-arm herself with her Chicago facade, however, a friendly voice called out.

"Well, well." A woman who could only be 'Mama' emerged from behind the counter, wiping her hands on an apron that read "EAT OR I'LL MAKE YOU." She was formidable, and seemed to occupy more space than the laws of physics should strictly allow. She was a vast, comforting landscape of a woman, with skin the color of well-steeped tea and eyes like polished obsidian that flickered with a sharp, unnerving intelligence. Her graying hair was scraped back into a knot so tight it gave her a look of permanent curiosity, and she possessed a bosom of such impressive proportions that Ava knew that she had been Mama or maybe even Granny to those younger than her since about the time she left high school. When she moved, it was with the practiced air of someone who had spent the last forty years successfully shushing the entire world into submission. She rustled with the sound of starched aprons and the faint hint of cinnamon. "You must be Beatrice's niece. City girl."

The way she said "city girl" made it sound like a diagnosis. *How did she know?* Small towns, no such thing as anonymity, thought Ava. They probably knew the moment I drove into town. "Ava Gardiner." She extended her hand. "And yes, I'm from Chicago."

The woman looked at her hand like it was a curious artifact, then shook it with a grip that could crack walnuts. "Claire Rossi. Everyone calls me Mama C. Take a seat, honey. You look like you need feeding."

Before Ava could protest, she found herself guided to a booth by the window. The other diners slowly resumed their meals, but she could still feel those eyes on her, assessing, judging, forming opinions.

"Coffee?" Mama C didn't wait for an answer, already pouring from a pot that looked older than Ava. "You're staying out at Beatrice's place."

It wasn't a question.

"For now. I'm fixing it up to sell" said Ava.

The coffee pot paused mid-pour. Around the diner, the temperature dropped several degrees as many pairs of ears latched onto her words.

"Sell." Mama C set the pot down with a definitive *thunk*. "That so?"

"Yeah, I'm an architect in Chicago so I'm using all my vacation and sick days to sort the place out before I go home. Willow Creek is a bit far to commute," she smiled, hoping it would catch on.

"Beatrice loved that house," Mama C said, ignoring Ava's thread of conversation and substituting her own. She pulled out a notepad. "Put her whole heart into it. Of course, she put her heart into a lot of things. People, mostly. Had a gift for seeing what folks needed before they knew it themselves." Mama C's eyes stayed fixed on Ava's.

Guilt twisted in Ava's stomach like a large knife. She lifted the coffee cup to hide her expression, and nearly gasped. It was perfect, strong and slightly sweet, exactly how she liked it, though she hadn't specified.

"How did you..." Ava began, but Mama C cut her off.

"Beatrice used to talk about you." Mama C's expression softened. "Said you worked too hard, cared too much, protected yourself too good. Said you took your coffee strong and sweet, just like you took your life, bitter with just enough hope to keep going."

Ava's throat tightened. She hadn't seen her aunt in years. Hadn't made time, hadn't thought it mattered. Now Aunt Bea was gone, and all Ava had were these strangers who seemed to have known her better than her own niece had. And worse, they seemed to know Ava like she was a long lost resident. "I'll have whatever's good," she managed to say through the growing lump in her throat.

"Everything's good, honey." Mama C chuckled. "But you look like you need comfort food." Mama C scribbled on her notepad. "Pancakes, bacon, eggs. Real eggs, from Betty Morrison's chickens. Real maple syrup." Mama C tucked her pencil behind her ear. "Liam treating you right out there?"

Mama C obviously didn't miss a beat, the question caught Ava off-guard. "He's... professional."

"Oooh, that man." Mama C shook her head, but there was warmth in it. "Took care of Beatrice like she was his own grandmother. Came by twice a week just to check on things, fix what needed fixing. Never took a dime. She left him her tools, you know. Her good ones. Made him promise to use them on the house, make sure whoever lived there next appreciated what she'd built."

Ava's chest constricted. Mama C obviously didn't believe in beating about the bush, but at the same time she came across as warm and caring, despite the very pointed and well directed line of conversation. "I didn't know," mumbled Ava.

"Lots you don't know, I'd wager." But Mama C's voice was gentle, not unkind. "That man's got the biggest heart in this county, even if he hides it under all that gruff. Whole town knows it. When the Parkers' barn burned down, who do you think rallied everyone to rebuild it? When Sarah Mitchell's husband ran off, who made sure her porch got fixed before winter? Liam McGregor looks out for his people."

His people. The phrase settled over Ava like a blanket she hadn't known she was missing. In Chicago, she had colleagues, contacts, and professional networks. But people? Her people? That list was painfully short.

"He's very dedicated," Ava said carefully.

Mama C's eyes twinkled. "Oh, honey. You've got that look."

"What look?" Ava asked, taken aback.

"The look every woman gets when she's trying real hard not to notice how that man fills out a flannel shirt." Mama C chuckled, and patted her hand. Ava fought hard not to blush. "Bless your heart, you're fighting a losing battle there. Trust me."

Heat flooded Ava's cheeks. "I'm not. We're not. I'm his employer" Ava said firmly.

"Mm-hmm." Mama C didn't look convinced. "I'll get your food."

Ava was mildly stunned, like she'd been hit very hard by a very nice and well meaning, but forceful storm of personality. As Mama C walked away, and Ava's mind swirled from the insinuations a man slid into the booth across from her, uninvited. He was probably in his sixties, lean and weathered, his white hair thinning but still holding on with a stubbornness that seemed to be part of the fabric of living in a small town. He had a look of someone who spent his days outdoors.

"Silas Thorne," he said, extending a calloused hand. "Postman. Also volunteer firefighter, occasional handyman, and full-time keeper of this town's secrets." He chuckled.

Despite feeling that she was being overwhelmed with introductions from strangers, Ava still managed a smile. "That's quite a resume."

"Small town. We all wear multiple hats." His eyes were sharp, assessing. "Heard you hired Liam for the renovation. Good choice. That man's a wizard with his hands."

"So everyone keeps telling me," Ava said.

"Course, he's got extra motivation with that house." Silas leaned back, casual as anything. "Beatrice was special to him. Used to have these long talks on her porch, late into the evening. She was like a grandmother to him."

"That sounds like Aunt Bea."

"She was friendly with everyone was our Beatrice. Kept to herself mainly, but was always friendly. Always ready with a kind ear and some advice or a good story. Loved her stories. Loved her advice too of course," he chuckled. "She was always writing. Stories. Letters. I was always bringing her mail from all over."

"Really," said Ava. "Didn't write me many letters."

Silas smiled. "Seemed like she was working on some project with all that writing. Very hush-hush. Wouldn't even let me peek, and I'm the postman! If you can't trust your postman, who can you trust?"

Ava realized he was fishing for a little gossip. Trying to see if she knew anything about these mysterious letters. She would have to leave him disappointed, and Ava was again reminded how little contact she had with Aunt Bea in recent years. "I haven't gone through much of her personal items yet," she said.

"Well." Silas stood, tipping an invisible hat. "If you find anything interesting, you let us know. Beatrice was a storyteller. Bet she left some good ones behind." He got up from the booth. "I'm sure I'll see you later" he said, and shuffled off.

Living in a small town meant everyone knew your business, a well known fact, even to a city-girl. But, apparently, Beatrice had managed to keep a little something to herself. Good for her, thought Ava. Maybe there was hope of personal space and secrets in a small town like this.

Mama C returned with a plate piled so high Ava couldn't see the table beneath it. "Eat up. You're too thin. City living'll do that to you. All stress, no substance."

Mama C's tone made it clear that eating was an order Ava couldn't refuse. She started with a pancake. The first bite melted on Ava's tongue, and she actually moaned. Fluffy, sweet, with real butter and maple syrup that tasted like liquid gold. The bacon was perfectly crispy. The eggs creamy and rich. "This is incredible," she said around another mouthful.

"Damn right it is." Mama C looked satisfied. "Food tastes better when it's made with love. Something your fancy city restaurants forget." Mama C clearly had no time for the city, but given how good her food was it was obviously the city's loss. Every bite was like a warm and comforting hug, and exactly what she hadn't known she needed.

She was scraping up the last of her syrup when the door chimed. She looked up automatically. Liam stood in the doorway, dust on his jeans, a smudge of something dark on his jaw. His eyes found hers, like he'd known exactly where she'd be.

"Liam!" Mama C called out. "Your usual?"

"Just coffee to go, Mama C. Got work waiting. Once I get some supplies at least," he said, not breaking eye contact with Ava. His voice was more teasing than anything else, like he fully expected her to have stopped here because it was part of some inevitable trap of Willow Creek's. He walked toward Ava's booth and stopped at the edge of her table. That smell of sawdust and soap again, and something essentially *him*. "Surviving?" he asked.

"Barely." She gestured at her empty plate. "I think Mama C's trying to fatten me up."

"Someone needs to." His eyes traced over her face, lingering on her mouth, and heat started to grow on her cheeks and neck. "You look like a strong wind could blow you away."

"I'm tougher than I look," said Ava defensively. *But nice to know he was looking at you*, said a voice at the back of her head. She quickly slammed the door on that thought.

"Mmmm," said Liam. The way he said it made her pulse skip.

Mama C appeared with a to-go cup, practically vibrating with glee. "Here you go, sweetheart. On the house."

Liam started to speak but Mama C stopped him.

"Hush. Consider it payment for taking care of our Ava here."

Our Ava. The phrase should've annoyed her. Instead, it settled somewhere warm behind her ribs, where that last pancake was.

"I should get to the hardware store," Ava said, suddenly desperate to escape the weight of Liam's gaze and Mama C's knowing smile. "I have that list of supplies."

"Remember to tell Dale I sent you," Liam said. "He'll only overcharge you by twenty percent."

"Gee, thanks."

His smile was slow and devastating. "Welcome to Willow Creek. Where everyone knows your business and no one lets you forget where you came from" he said, heading for the door.

He left before she could formulate a response, the door chiming behind him. Through the window, she watched him climb into his truck, and hated how her eyes followed the movement of his shoulders, the way his hair curled at his collar.

"Honey," Mama C said, sauntering over to her. "Let me give you some advice. Free of charge." Before Ava could respond, she continued. "That man out there? He's going to break down every wall you've got. Question is, are you brave enough to let him?"

Ava's throat went tight. "I don't need my walls broken down," she said defensively. They're there for a reason she added to herself. You need walls in Chicago. Walls are good.

"I'm sure." Mama C's expression was impossibly kind. "But Beatrice didn't leave you this house just so you could sell it, honey. She left it so you could find something you've been missing. Maybe that's peace. Maybe that's purpose." She paused. "Maybe it's a six-foot-two contractor with a hero complex and eyes that could melt steel."

Despite everything, the ridiculousness of the suggestion and the absurd thought of Aunt Bea playing matchmaker with her and Liam, Ava laughed. "You're terrible."

"I'm a romantic. And I know a love story when I see one starting." Mama C stood, patting Ava's shoulder. "Now go get your supplies. And when you come back through, because you will come back through, I'll have pie waiting. Cherry, just like Beatrice used to like."

Ava sat in the driver's seat of the rental, the engine idling with a rhythmic purr that felt increasingly like a foreign language in the dust-choked parking lot of Miller's Hardware. Outside, the air smelled of manure; inside, the climate control was locked at a crisp sixty-eight degrees, filtered and familiar.

She pressed her phone to her ear, the plastic warm against her skin. "I can't do it, Maya. I'm staring at a storefront that has a hand-painted sign for 'Live Bait' sitting next to a display of industrial-grade shop vacs. I feel like I've accidentally driven onto the set of a survivalist documentary."

Maya's voice came through dripping with sympathy. "Then don't do it, babe. You're sitting in a car, just put it in reverse and get the builder to go get his own supplies. Better yet, just come home and let him finish it himself, he clearly has his own vision for what he wants this place to be, let him get on with it."

"I can't," Ava hissed, glancing at her reflection in the rearview mirror. She looked frayed, her blowout was losing its battle against the mountain humidity. "If I go back now, Martin wins. That job wins. I'm stuck there forever. And if I leave Builder Boy alone he'll spend months restoring the cottage to a museum piece that will eat my budget and no one will want to buy. Not for the money I want."

"You're not stuck forever," Maya countered. "Think about tonight. If you were here, we'd be at that little place on Dearborn. You wouldn't be worrying about subfloors or bait, you'd be deciding between the Malbec and the Cabernet. Your barista at the Starbucks on the corner probably thinks you've been kidnapped. He saw me this morning and actually asked if you wanted your usual caramel macchiato with the extra shot. He's holding it for you, Ava."

Ava closed her eyes. She could almost taste it. The burnt, sophisticated bitterness of the coffee, the way the steam touched her face as she drank it in the air-conditioned lobby of her office.

"And lunch," Maya continued, her voice a siren song of urban comfort. "I walked past the silver hot dog van on 4th, the one with the vendor who knows exactly how much of that spicy brown mustard you like. He asked where the 'Power Suit' was. Chicago misses you. Everything here is easy, everything there is... plywood."

"It's not plywood," Ava said, though her resolve was wavering. "It's 'Good Bones.' That's what Liam called it. He's back at the house right now, measuring the kitchen like he's performing surgery. His only instructions are not to buy the 'cheap stuff.' He thinks I'm a tourist, Maya. He's just waiting for me to realize I don't belong here."

"You don't!" Maya laughed, but it wasn't unkind. "This is going to be a long thirty days, I know, but just remember you belong where the streets are paved and the mustard is spicy. In a world where you don't have to know the difference between a Phillips head and a flathead. And when you get back we can go get our nails done. You're bleeding under your cuticles, Ava. I can hear it in your voice."

Ava looked out at the hardware store. A man in overalls was loading bags of concrete into a rusted truck, moving with a slow, deliberate pace that felt like a personal insult to her thirty day timeline. Everything in Willow Creek moved like molasses, and she was the only one trying to outrun the winter. She looked at the scrap of paper Liam had given her. His handwriting was surprisingly neat, all caps, bold and steady. 'Don't get the plastic shims. Get the cedar.'

"He said if we don't do it right, we don't do it at all," Ava mused. "He's back there probably expecting me to come back with the wrong nails just so he can give me that 'I told you so' look. He called it 'The McGregor Way.'"

"Sounds like a recipe for a headache," Maya let out an exasperated sigh on Ava's behalf. "The Starbucks way is much more your vibe."

Ava took a breath. She thought about the caramel macchiato and the spicy mustard. She thought about the clean, glass-and-steel perfection of her old life. Then she thought about the way the cottage had groaned when she stepped on the threshold, not in protest, but in welcome. The nice molding she liked.

"I'm hanging up now," Ava said with conviction, her hand reaching for the door handle. "If I'm not back in Chicago in twenty-seven days, you can have my espresso machine."

"Ava—"

"I have to buy the cedar shims, Maya. If I don't, the carpenter wins." She hung up the phone, killed the car, and marched towards the hardware to the sound of her loafers crunching on the stones and the caw of a distant crow.

Miller's Hardware smelled like motor oil, cut wood, and fertilizer, a sharp contrast to the sweet warmth of the diner, but better than the manure outside. Ava found herself in a maze of shelves stacked floor to ceiling with everything from nails to chainsaws. A middle aged man emerged from the back, wiping his hands on a rag. "Help you?" he asked.

"Liam McGregor sent me. I need supplies for a renovation." She pulled out the scrap of paper with the list Liam had written out. Professional-grade drywall, primer, paint, brushes, drop cloths, spackling compound...

The man, his name tag read "Dale" peered at her list and whistled. "Doing it right, huh? This for Beatrice's place?"

"Yes." *Does everyone know my business?* she thought.

"Liam doing the work?"

"Yes."

Dale's weathered face split into a grin. "Then you're in good hands. Best carpenter in three counties. Let me pull this for you."

As he moved through the store, gathering items, Silas materialized from what appeared to be thin air. "Told you I'd see you later" he chuckled. "Dale taking care of you?"

"Very efficiently."

"That's not the Willow Creek way." Silas was carrying a small can of wood stain and stood, legs apart, one hand in his pocket in a comfortable slouch like he was settling in for a chat. "We like to take our time, make sure you get exactly what you need. Can't do that if you're rushing."

Ava glanced at her watch. A mistake.

"Got somewhere to be?" Silas asked, amused.

"I was hoping to get back and..."

"Help Liam?" He grinned. "Honey, that man works better when he's got thinking time. Trust me. Rushing him is like trying to rush spring. It'll come when it comes."

Dale returned with a cart piled high. "This should do you. Liam said you wanted the good stuff, so that's what I got. None of that big-box-store garbage."

Ava looked at the small heap and tried not to wince with thoughts of the cost. But the quality was evident in every item, and something about supporting local businesses felt right to her in a way her usual Amazon orders never had. She and Dale made their way to the counter to settle up, Silas following along behind.

As Dale was tallying the bill, Silas leaned against the counter, his weathered hands tracing the edge of a color sample. "Beatrice, Mama C, and I, we'd spend hours right here debating crown molding profiles and whether buttercream was too yellow." His voice softened. "Bea had such plans for that cottage. Wanted to restore every inch." He paused, clearing his throat. "Liam tried everything, came by twice a week with wood samples, sketches. But she got sick so fast." His eyes met Ava's, bright with unshed tears. "Breaks my heart she never got to see it finished. Would've meant the world to her. She'd be happy you're using the good stuff that's for sure."

Ava could only nod and give a weak smile.

As Dale loaded her car for her, which was completely impractical for hauling supplies, as Liam had undoubtedly known, Silas appeared again at her elbow. "One more thing," he said quietly. "About those letters I mentioned. If you do find anything, maybe... maybe look at them before you decide what to do with the house. Beatrice had her reasons for everything. I think she wanted you to understand."

"Understand what?" Ava inquired. But Silas just smiled, nodded, and wandered away, leaving Ava with more questions than answers.

The drive back to the cottage felt different. The landscape that had seemed charming on the way in was now almost alive with possibility. What secrets had Aunt Beatrice been keeping? What had she and Liam talked about on those long evenings? And why did it matter so much to a town full of strangers? When she pulled up to the cottage, her car now dusty and undignified, she found the front door open. Music drifted out, classic rock, played low. Inside, Liam had transformed the living room. The old drywall was gone, replaced by fresh boards. Drop cloths covered the floor, and he stood on a ladder, measuring something on the ceiling.

He looked down when she entered, and his face did something complicated. Relief? Something warmer she didn't want to name? A small crack in the grumpy facade though. "Successful trip?" he asked.

"I was interrogated by a postman, adopted by a diner owner, and convinced to buy supplies I'm not entirely sure we need."

His laugh was low and genuine. "Sounds right. Welcome to small-town commerce."

Ava set down her purse and, before she could think better of it, grabbed the other end of the board he was positioning. "Where does this go?"

Liam's eyes widened slightly. "You don't have to..."

"I know, but you need labor, remember? Besides, I want to." And she realized, with a start, that she meant it.

They worked in an almost comfortable silence, Liam calling out measurements, Ava holding boards steady and chirping about saleability, Liam grunting about respecting the workmanship. Then they would fall silent and repeat the process moments later. On the whole, though, an uneasy truce seemed to be forming in the battle of saving vs selling the cottage. Their hands would accidentally brush from time to time as they passed tools, and each touch sent sparks racing up Ava's arms. Over time, the space between them hummed with banter and with unspoken things, attraction, yes, but also something deeper. Understanding, maybe. Recognition?

"Mama C said you took care of Aunt Beatrice. That the whole town thinks you're some kind of hero." Ava said it before she could stop herself.

"Did she now?" Liam's voice was carefully neutral but there was a tightness back in his jaw, Ava could tell. He climbed down from the ladder, his expression unreadable. "Mama C exaggerates."

"Does she?" Ava stepped closer, drawn by something she couldn't name. "Or do you just not like people seeing who you really are?"

They were mere inches apart now. The flecks of gold in his hazel eyes caught the light and seemed to sparkle. The heat radiating from his body after hours of work evidence of the raw power of the man. It was only a second, but it lasted a full century. Before either could speak a knock at the door shattered the moment. They jumped apart like guilty teenagers.

Silas stood on the porch, holding a casserole dish. "Am I interrupting something?"

"No," Ava and Liam chorused, with a speed that would rival light.

Silas smiled a knowing smile. "Mama C sent this. Said you need real food, not just hardware store coffee and determination." He looked between them, then handed over the casserole dish.

Ava's face burned. "Nothing's..." she began.

"Happening" finished Liam. "We're just..."

Silas chuckled. "Beatrice said her niece needed someone to show her that walls were meant to have doors. Don't let me get in the way, I can see you've got lots to do. Mama C said you can drop the dish off any time." And Silas was already heading back to the gate, his hand (Ava noticed) reaching for the phone in his pocket.

"Dammit!" cursed Liam. "Gossip's gonna be all through town within the next hour."

"Do small towns really work that...hang on! Why are you so worried about gossip spreading?" Ava said with shock, catching up to his meaning.

Liam gave her the side eye. "No offense, I'm sure you're a real catch in Chicago, but I could do without half the town creating stories about me and whatever stray women drift through town."

Ava's mouth formed a perfect O. "I'll have you know I'm a catch anywhere. And 'stray woman?!'" She mentally kicked herself for picking up the insult a moment too late.

"Well, fly in, fly out...flighty then?"

Avas O doubled in size. "I'm not flighty!" she crossed her arms, her voice rising.

"Oh you're right. Thirty days. What was I thinking?" He grunted with a half laugh.

"If anyone should be concerned about gossip it's me," said Ava, trying to regain the high ground.

"Right. So we are both concerned about the same thing," said Liam with the tone of a man who had no idea he'd said wrong, and was glad Ava had caught up to be on the same page about their mutual concern.

"!" Ava exclaimed. "Yes but...that's not...the point is... I'm desirable anywhere outside of Chicago."

"OK" Liam said noncommittally and began gathering his tools.

Ava stood there, bewildered, still forming a (slightly smaller) O, unsure how she managed to lose an argument where they both agreed that town gossip was something neither wanted. She was used to boardrooms and could hold her own with any misogynistic opinionated man out there. How did Liam McGregor get her frazzled?

I'm not flighty, I just have a deadline. And a great life to get home to. Where everyone finds me attractive.

It was the perfect comeback. Unfortunately she thought of it 10 seconds after Liam had left for the night, saying "see you at six."

She stood, alone, in the middle of the room looking for a positive to claim for herself. Well...she had the casserole, so she was definitely putting this down as a victory for her. Take that, McGregor.

It did not make her feel any better.

The Wall

The alarm hadn't even gone off yet.

Ava stared at the ceiling of the guest bedroom. Her bedroom now, she supposed. She watched the pre-dawn light creep across the plaster medallion overhead. The emotions of last night were still a hot memory.

It was a good casserole. Mama C was a great cook.

Liam's grumpy exterior, scowling and the way he was more concerned people would think he was interested in her than the other way around, didn't line up in her head with the gentleness he could put in his voice and the skill and love he could show working with wood. How dare he call her flighty! And he should be so lucky to have her interested in him. She should be the one offended by the threat of gossip, but she was actually offended by the fact that he was taking more offense than she was, as if liking her was the worst thing in the world. It was offensive. Argh! He annoyed her like few others. She didn't know the first thing about the country and country men and was grateful for it. Her life was Chicago, with Starbucks and skyscrapers...and debts and bills...

You didn't mind the suggestion of Liam when Mama C hinted at it in the diner yesterday teased the voice in her head. "That was before I knew he was against it" she said back, and pushed those unwanted thoughts back into the darkness of her mind where they belonged.

Outside, a bird she couldn't name was singing its heart out, oblivious to the fact that it was barely five-thirty in the morning. Her entire body ached. Not the sharp pain of injury, but the deep, bone-level soreness that came from using muscles she'd forgotten existed. Her shoulders protested as she pushed herself upright. Her thighs burned as she swung her legs out of bed. Even her hands were stiff, the soft skin of her palms were tender from yesterday's work stripping wallpaper in the upstairs hallway. She'd done Pilates three times a week in Chicago. She'd thought she was in decent shape. She was wrong.

Ava padded to the bathroom and flicked on the light, wincing at her reflection. Her dark hair was a disaster, still carrying traces of plaster dust despite last night's shower. There were shadows under her eyes that her usual concealer wouldn't touch, and when she lifted her arms to tie her hair back, she saw the beginnings of bruises along her forearms, souvenirs from wrestling an antique dresser down the stairs by herself last night because she stubbornly wasn't going to ask Liam to help this morning. She looked like someone who worked with her hands. The thought was strange. But not entirely unpleasant.

By the time she made it downstairs, dressed in her newest uniform of yoga pants and an old college sweatshirt, she'd managed to scrape her hair into a ponytail and splash enough cold water on her face to feel almost human. The work boots sat by the back door where she'd left them last night, sturdy, steel-toed things Dale had sold her. They were nothing like the sleek leather ankle boots caked in mud and now gathering dust in her closet upstairs. Ava laced them up slowly, her fingers clumsy on the thick laces. The boots were heavy, practical, and deeply unsexy. They made her feel like she was playing dress-up, pretending to be someone who knew what they were doing. Which, to be fair, she absolutely was.

The cottage was quiet around her in that particular way old houses had, not silent, exactly, but full of small sounds. The tick of the radiator. The creak of floorboards settling. The faint whisper of wind against the windowpanes. Ava moved through the kitchen, starting the coffee maker Liam had dug out of storage for her. While it gurgled and hissed, she found herself noticing things she'd been too overwhelmed to see before. The way the early morning light slanted through the east-facing windows, catching the beveled edge of the glass and throwing tiny rainbows across the wall. The craftsmanship of the crown molding, each piece hand-carved, fitted together like a puzzle she had liked on the first day, but now adored in this light. The wide-plank floors that had been worn smooth by generations of footsteps. Beatrice had loved this place. Liam had said it yesterday, his voice rough with something that might have been grief, and Ava had brushed past it in her eagerness to start making plans. Now, standing alone in the morning quiet, she could almost feel it—the weight of all that love, soaked into the bones of the house.

The coffee finished brewing just as she heard movement outside. Liam, right on schedule at six AM. She poured herself a cup and tried not to think about the fact that she was already learning his routines. He appeared at the doorway holding his thermos and a yellow bundle of fabric. She turned to look at him and he held her gaze for a second before saying "I brought you this" and held the bundle towards her.

"I thought small town folks were big on pleasantries. Like 'good mornin' Miss Gardiner.'" Ava sipped her coffee, and didn't reach for the fabric.

"Yes. Right. Morning," he looked almost abashed at having forgotten. "Barnaby down!" Barnaby had bounded into the room, around Liam and made a beeline for Ava. She put her coffee down and bent to give him a hug.

"Good morning Barnaby, who's a good dog?" She played with his ears and ruffled his coat. After ignoring Liam and leaving him for a few more moments, she considered it was time to acknowledge his offering. "What is it?" she asked, taking the bundle from him. Unfolding it, she realised it was flannel, a large yellow flannel shirt like the ones he wore.

"I figured you probably have limited clothing choices for this work in your thirty day Chicago wardrobe. Brought you a spare of mine" he said.

Today, he was wearing a green flannel to match her yellow. "What? Do you have one in every color?"

"Not orange."

"Oh of course not, not with your skin tone."

"No, I just can't find it in orange."

Ava smiled despite herself and memories of last night. Liam's lips moved slightly in a way that Ava was learning was as close to a smile as he got. Damn, she thought, but said "thanks."

"Don't mention it."

"Coffee?"

"Please."

Barnaby stood between them wagging his tail. She poured him a cup and he rested his thermos on the counter. *Off to a good start today. Maybe it will be smooth sailing from here.*

"Absolutely not."

Liam stood in the doorway between the kitchen and dining room, arms crossed, looking at Ava like she'd just suggested they burn the house down for the insurance money.

"It's the best option," Ava insisted, gesturing at the wall behind her. "Open concept is what buyers want. Kitchen, dining, living—all one big entertaining space. It would completely transform the flow of the first floor."

"It's not that, it's the wall. It's load-bearing."

"You can't know that for sure."

"I know buildings," he said incredulously. "I know this house. My grandfather built this addition. That wall isn't decorative, Ava. It's holding up the second floor."

Ava pulled out her phone, scrolling to the research she'd compiled last night. "But according to the comparable sales data, homes with open floor plans sell for an average of fifteen percent more than..."

Liam cut her off, his voice flat, he jaw clenched. "You want to knock out a load-bearing wall? Fine. We bring in an engineer, get proper plans drawn up, install a steel beam. That's going to cost at least fifteen thousand and push our timeline back three weeks."

"We don't have three weeks!" Ava was more disappointed than anything else. "We need to make this place market-ready in three weeks. You know that."

They stared at each other across the narrow kitchen, the late morning light harsh on both their faces. Ava noticed that Liam looked like he'd slept even less than she had, his dark hair rumpled and a shadow of stubble along his jaw. She hated that she'd noticed.

"There's something wrong with the central beam," Liam said finally, his voice quieter now. "I could feel it yesterday when we were working upstairs. The whole house is settling unevenly. If we take out that wall without proper support..."

"Well, let's look at it," Ava interrupted. "Let's make a small opening and see what we're actually dealing with. Maybe there is a way we can make things work. Without the three weeks."

"I'm not wrong," he said quickly.

"Let's just see."

There was a pause and then he turned and disappeared into what Beatrice had called the "mudroom", a cluttered space off the kitchen by the back door that seemed to function as Liam's tool storage. He returned carrying a sledgehammer, its handle worn smooth with use.

"Fine," he said, holding it out to her. "You want to open the wall? Open it. But you're doing the work."

Ava looked at the sledgehammer. It was heavier than she'd expected, the weight of it settling into her hands with a solid, undeniable reality. She fought the urge to put it down so she could show Liam how strong she was. "I don't know what I'm doing," she admitted.

Something shifted in Liam's expression, not quite a smile, but a softening around the edges. "I know. That's why I'm going to teach you. Just like the pry bar. And for God's sake don't let go of this one."

The wall, up close, looked more substantial than it had from across the room. Liam made her put on safety glasses and gloves, which made her feel both more professional and more ridiculous. He'd marked out a section of drywall about three feet square, using a level to make sure the lines were straight. "You want to start with a test hole," he explained, standing close enough that she could feel the warmth of him at her shoulder. "Small and controlled. We see what's behind the drywall before we commit to anything bigger."

"Okay." Ava's voice came out steadier than she would admit she was. The sledgehammer was heavy in her hands. Remembering the pry bar, she gripped it tight.

"Don't overthink it," Liam said. "Trust your body. Let the weight of the hammer do the work."

He stepped behind her then, and Ava's breath caught as his hands closed over hers on the handle. His chest was a solid wall of heat at her back, his arms bracketing hers as he adjusted her grip.

"Like this," he murmured, his voice low and close to her ear. "Hands apart for leverage. Knees bent. Swing from your core, not your arms."

Ava couldn't think. Every nerve in her body was focused on the points where Liam was touching her. His breath stirring the loose hairs at her temple, the solid presence of him surrounding her like a force field.

"Got it?" he asked.

She nodded, not trusting her voice.

Liam stepped back, and the sudden absence of his warmth was a noticeable loss. Ava forced herself to focus on the wall, on the marked square of drywall, on the weight of the sledgehammer in her hands. She swung.

The impact reverberated up her arms, through her shoulders, into her teeth. The sledgehammer made a small dent in the drywall and bounced back.

"From the core. *Not* your arms," Liam reminded her.

She tried again, this time putting her entire body into it. The impact again reverberated through her body, but this time the sledgehammer punched through the drywall with a satisfying crack. For one glorious moment, Ava felt powerful. Capable. Like she could demolish anything that stood in her path. Another swing, bits of drywall falling away. Sledgehammers were fun, she could get used to this. Another swing. Another. She was getting the hang of this and the opening in the wall was now substantial, and all of it had been plaster. Overconfident, she swung again to make the gap wider. But this time she connected with something much more solid than drywall.

The house groaned.

It was a sound unlike anything Ava had ever heard, a deep, wooden protest that seemed to come from the very bones of the structure. Above them, a crack appeared in the plaster, fine dust raining down like snow.

"Move!" Liam's shout cut through her shock. "Now!"

She was frozen, staring up at the ceiling as it visibly sank, ancient timbers creaking in warning. Then Liam was there, his body slamming into hers, shoving her backward as he lunged forward. He squeezed himself into the hole she'd made in the plaster and braced himself under the sagging ceiling, arms raised. Ava watched in horror as he took the weight of the failing structure on his shoulders.

"The jack!" he gritted out, his face contorted with effort. "In the mudroom. Red handle. Now!"

Her body unlocked. She ran. The adjustable jack-post was exactly where he'd said, leaning against the wall with a dozen other tools she couldn't name. It was heavy, awkward in her hands, but adrenaline made her strong. She dragged it back to the kitchen, her heart hammering so hard she could feel it in her throat. Liam was where she'd left him, arms shaking with the effort of holding up the ceiling. His face had gone pale, tendons standing out in his neck.

"Under my arm," he said, his voice strained. "You need to get the jack positioned directly below the beam. Can you see it?"

Ava could. Through the hole in the wall, a massive central post, ancient wood that had held this house together for over a century, had started to buckle. She had managed to knock it on her last blow, just enough to be the straw on the camel's back of a process decades in the making. She dropped to her knees and crawled forward, into the narrow space between Liam's body and the wall. It was tight, so tight that she had to press herself against him to fit, her back to his chest, his arm braced above her head.

"Good," Liam breathed, and she could feel the word rumble through his chest. "Now lift the jack. Straight up. Until it touches the beam." His sentences were short and sharp, the effort of bracing the ceiling evident.

Ava's hands were shaking so badly she could barely grip the metal. She raised the jack, inch by inch, feeling the weight of it increase as it made contact with the ceiling. Liam's other hand came down to help her, his fingers wrapping around hers on the adjustment handle.

"Now turn," he said, his voice right in her ear. "Clockwise. Slow and steady."

Together, they turned the handle. The jack extended, taking the weight on the overhead beam, and Ava saw the moment the pressure eased off Liam's shoulders as his breath came out in a shuddering exhale that stirred her hair.

"Keep going," he murmured. "Just a little more."

They turned the handle again, and again, until the jack was fully engaged and the ceiling had stopped its terrifying descent. Only then did Liam lower his arms, his body sagging slightly against hers.

They were both breathing hard, pressed together in the narrow space beneath the compromised beam. Ava could feel every point of contact between them, the solid wall of his chest against her back, his thighs bracketing hers, his heartbeat thundering against her shoulder blade. He smelled like sawdust and sweat and something masculine that made her want to turn in his arms and...

"Are you okay?" Liam asked, and his voice was rough, strained with more than just physical effort.

"I think so." Ava's own voice came out barely above a whisper. "Are you?"

"Yeah." He didn't move away. Neither did she. "That was close."

"I'm sorry. God, Liam, I'm so sorry. You were right, and I didn't listen, and I could have..."

"Hey." His hand found her shoulder, squeezed gently. "You didn't do it on purpose. And when it mattered, you stayed."

Ava looked up at him. His face was inches from hers, close enough to read the pattern of the gold flecks in his hazel eyes, the fine lines that crinkled at the corners. "Of course I stayed," she said. "I wasn't going to let you hold up the house by yourself."

His eyes flashed surprise, maybe, or something deeper. It made her stomach flip. His gaze dropped to her mouth, and Ava's breath caught.

For one suspended moment, neither of them moved.

Then Liam cleared his throat and pulled back, breaking the spell. "We should get away from the wall," he said, his voice carefully neutral. "Just in case."

"Right. Yes. Good idea."

They extracted themselves from the narrow space with considerably less grace than they'd entered it. By the time they were both standing in the relative safety of the kitchen, her face was red hot and her heart was still racing for reasons that had nothing to do with the near-disaster. Liam ran a hand through his hair, leaving it standing up in dark spikes. "I need to get more jacks," he said, not quite meeting her eyes. "Shore up the whole beam before anything else comes down." He shook his head. "This will take some work."

"How bad?" Ava asked.

"Bad enough I think we're going to need a structural engineer out here. They may be able to secure the beam without substantial work if we can support this main post. I don't think Miller's can get a steel joist but maybe..." He looked around at the damaged wall, at the jack holding up their ceiling, at the mess of plaster and drywall dust coating everything. Ava wanted to argue. Wanted to pull out her data and her projections and find a way to make this less of a disaster. But she'd swung that sledgehammer. She'd seen the crack in the beam, heard the house groan under the weight of its own history.

"Okay," she said. "What do we do first?"

Liam looked at her then, really looked at her, and something in his expression made her chest tight. "You're not going to fight me on this?"

"You saved me...the house, you saved the house," Ava stammered. "I think I can trust you to know what comes next."

He held her gaze for a long moment, and Ava began to be pulled in again by that strange gravitational force that seemed to exist in the space between them. Then Liam nodded, just once, and offered her his hand. "Come on," he said. "Let's clean up this mess."

His palm was rough and warm against hers as he pulled her to her feet. Ava told herself the flutter in her stomach was just residual adrenaline.

She was getting very good at lying to herself.

It was Ava who rediscovered it.

They'd been working for the better part of an hour, carefully clearing debris from around the damaged wall while Liam installed additional support jacks, carefully expanding the hole to get around the broken post to add more support on the other side of the beam. The physical labor was almost meditative. Bend, lift, carry, dump, repeat. Her body had settled into the rhythm of it, the soreness from earlier forgotten in the face of this new, focused work.

Kneeling on the floor, sweeping plaster dust into a dustpan, when she saw the flash of color near the baseboard.

The old tin box from the day before.

In the excitement of the busted pipe, she had forgotten all about it. But here it was, wedged into a gap between the wall and the floor, in a space once hidden by the old baseboard. She set down the dustpan and reached in, tugging gently. It came free slowly, reluctant to give up its hiding place. "Hey I forgot about this," she called to Liam. "What is it?"

He crossed the room to crouch beside her, his shoulder brushing hers as he leaned in to look. "That's... huh."

Around the tin, unseen in the glimpse she'd had before, was an old silk scarf. It was beautiful, though the silk was slightly brittle with age it was still lustrous. Ava spread it across her lap, marveling at the craftsmanship. Hand-rolled edges. A delicate pattern of flowers she didn't recognize.

Opening the tin, she found it contained a bundle wrapped in waxed paper. The paper crackled as she unfolded it, revealing a stack of letters, the envelopes yellowed with age.

Ava's breath caught. "Are those..."

"Love letters," Liam finished, he took the top envelope, his eyes scanning for details. The handwriting was elegant, old-fashioned, addressed to 'Dearest B'.

They looked at each other, kneeling in the wreckage of the wall they'd torn down, holding pieces of someone else's story. The afternoon light slanted across them, illuminating the dust motes dancing in the air, and Ava felt the strangest sensation, like the house was sharing its secrets with them, trusting them with something precious.

Outside, that unnamed bird was still singing, and somewhere in the bones of Beatrice's house, a wall between them finally began to crumble.

The Little Tin Box

The letters smelled of lavender and time.

Ava sat cross-legged on the kitchen floor, the packet of yellowed envelopes resting in her lap like something fragile and holy. The paper had weight and substance between her fingers, not the cheap copy paper of her marketing proposals, but thick, textured stock that had been expensive once. The kind of paper you bought when words mattered. When they were meant to last.

She could still feel the phantom ache in her palms from the sledgehammer, still taste the dust from the wall's collapse settling in her throat, but those sensations seemed distant now. Muted. The world had contracted to this: the weight of the letters, the faded ink visible through the translucent envelope, and the absolute stillness that had fallen over the kitchen.

Ava looked up to Liam kneeling next to her. "We should read them," she said softly. Her voice came out rougher than she'd expected, scraped raw by more than just the dust. "Don't you think? I mean, we found them. Maybe we're supposed to..."

"No."

The word came out sharp, almost harsh, but when Ava's eyes snapped to his face, she saw something complicated flickering there. Not anger. Something deeper. "No?" she repeated.

Liam exhaled slowly, then he stood and crossed to the kitchen window overlooking the tangled garden, and stood there with his back to her, his shoulders tight beneath the worn fabric of his flannel shirt. "They're not ours," he said finally. "Those letters. They weren't meant for us."

Ava looked down at the packet again. The top envelope was addressed in looping, old-fashioned script: *Dearest B.* No last name. No address. Just that single, intimate initial. "But Beatrice is gone," Ava said gently. "And whoever wrote these, they're probably gone too. I mean, these have to be at least fifty years old or more. This isn't just old, this is *history*."

"Exactly." He turned back to face her, and the expression on his face made something twist in Ava's chest. He looked... wounded. Like she'd touched a nerve she hadn't known existed. "It's her history. Her private history. And she hid these in the wall for a reason."

"Or she lost them," Ava countered, but even as she said it, she wasn't sure she believed it. The silk scarf, the careful placement beneath the baseboard, it looked deliberate. Intentional. She changed tack. "Maybe she meant for someone to find them someday. Maybe that's why she kept them in the first place."

Liam was quiet for a long moment. Then, to Ava's surprise, he crossed back to where she sat and lowered himself to the floor beside her. Not close, there was still a careful distance between them, but close enough that she could smell that sawdust and pine.

"You didn't know her," he said quietly. His eyes were fixed on the letters in her lap, and there was something in his expression that made Ava's breath catch. "Beatrice, I mean. You didn't know what kind of person she was."

"No," Ava admitted. "I didn't. I only saw her a few times a year a long time ago. But I know she was sweet. Kind. I know she...would have liked to see me more."

A small, sharp muscle pulsed in the hollow of his cheek, the only sign that he was trying to grind his words into dust. Finally he said "she was all of those things. But she was also private. Fiercely private. She didn't talk about herself, not really. Not about the things that mattered."

Ava studied his profile, the straight line of his nose, the sharp angle of his jaw, the way a muscle jumped there when he was holding something back. "But she talked to you," she said softly. It wasn't a question.

He was silent for so long that Ava thought he wouldn't answer. Then the words started to fall between them like stones into still water, rippling outward with implications Ava didn't fully understand yet. "She did. I fixed things for her, sure," Liam's voice low and careful. "But we also... talked. A lot. She'd make tea, that god-awful chamomile stuff that tasted like lawn clippings, and we'd sit on the porch or at that table." He nodded toward the old dining set pushed against the far wall, the one Ava had already mentally replaced with something mid-century modern. "And she'd tell me stories."

"Stories about what?"

"About the house. About the town, back when it was different. Smaller. About the people who used to live here." He paused, and when he spoke again, his voice had softened even further. "About the man she loved."

Ava's heart kicked hard against her ribs. "The man who wrote these letters?"

"Maybe. Probably." Liam reached out, hesitated, then gently took the top envelope from the stack in her lap. His fingers were careful, reverent almost, as he turned it over in his hands. He closed his eyes. "It was my grandfather. They could never be together. Not directly. But she talked about him like... like he was still with her and part of her life, you know? Like the years hadn't passed at all. Like she could still feel him in every corner of this house."

The ache in Ava's chest intensified. "Why couldn't they be together?" she asked.

"This town used to be different, back when they were young" Liam said. He set the envelope back down carefully, his gaze distant. "Smaller. More... rigid. People knew their place, and they stuck to it. Beatrice's family had money, not a lot, but enough that it mattered. Enough that they had expectations."

"And he didn't have money?"

"He was a woodworker." Something shifted in Liam's expression, pride, maybe, mixed with old grief. "He made furniture. Beautiful stuff. Chairs and tables that would last generations. But he worked with his hands, and back then, that meant something different. It meant you were working class. It meant you weren't good enough for a girl like Beatrice Hartley."

Ava's throat tightened. She looked down at the letters again, at that careful, looping script. *To My Dearest B.* How many times had he written those words? How many letters had he penned, knowing they could never be sent through normal channels? Knowing they had to be hidden, treasured in secret, kept like contraband?

"So they met in secret," she said softly. "Here? In this house?"

"No, no, nothing like that," he said quickly, and Ava was embarrassed for having suggested Liam's grandfather and her Aunt Bea had some sort of clandestine affair. "They were respectable people. Each of them married someone else, and Grandad Thomas and Grandma Elsie were together until the end. But still, there was a love between them of a sort. An eternal, very close friendship and closeness. Even if they couldn't actually be together. He worked on this house, which gave them time together. Every piece of custom woodwork, the built-in shelves, the window seats, the crown molding, he made all of it. For her. And he'd give her little wooden trinkets he'd carved, flowers from the meadow beyond town. But they'd mostly live in letters, where they'd plan and live a life they both knew they'd never have."

The grief in his voice was so raw, so present, that Ava found herself reaching out before she'd consciously decided to move. Her hand found his where it rested on his knee, and she squeezed gently. He didn't pull away.

"How do you know all this?" she asked.

"She told me." Liam turned his hand over beneath hers, his calloused palm warm against her fingers. "After my grandfather died, one of his wishes was that I would look after Beatrice's house. It was special to him, he said. Over time Beatrice and I grew close and eventually she shared about the love she and my grandfather never had."

"That's why you know this house so well," Ava said wonderingly. "Because your grandfather built half of it."

"More than half." Liam's smile was small and sad. "And when things broke or wore out, Beatrice would call me. Because I was Thomas's grandson, and she knew I'd fix things the way he would have wanted. The way he would have done, if he'd still been here."

Things started to make a lot more sense now in Ava's mind. The way Liam had touched the exposed beams with such reverence. The careful attention he paid to every piece of original woodwork, every door frame and window sill. The anger, no, not anger, *pain* in his eyes when she'd suggested ripping things out and starting fresh.

"He died when I was 19," said Liam. "But before that, he taught me everything. How to read wood grain, how to feel for weakness in a joint, how to make something that would outlast the person who built it." His voice roughened. "He taught me that every piece of wood has a story, and it's a craftsman's job to honor that. To work with it, not against it."

"I understand," Ava said quietly. Understanding tinged with shame. "When I wanted to gut the place. When I talked about open-concept and granite and...I'm so sorry. I didn't know." She withdrew her hand and held her face in her hands. What must he think of me? She thought.

"How could you?" He looked at her finally, really looked at her, and as their eyes met the intensity in his gray eyes made her breath catch. "I never told you. I just... I saw another out-of-towner coming in with big plans and no respect for what was already here. I assumed you were just like all the others that pass through this place."

"Maybe I was," Ava admitted. The words hurt to say, but they rang true. "Maybe I still am. I mean, I still need to sell this place. I still need the money." Ava looked down at the letters scattered across her lap, at the gap in the wall where afternoon light now poured through. She thought about her tablet, currently buried somewhere in her bag, with its neat spreadsheet of projected profits and renovation costs. About the schedule on the fridge and where they should be up to. She thought about the two bedrooms in Chicago she'd already started browsing online, the sleek high-rise with the doorman and the city views.

"I don't know," she said finally. Honestly. "I just know that sitting here, holding these letters, thinking about your grandfather and Beatrice and everything they couldn't have... The house feels different. Like it's not just walls and floors and potential anymore. It's..."

"A story," Liam finished. "Don't get that in Chicago."

"Mmmm."

They sat for a long moment in silence. Sitting here with these letters, with the weight of two lives lived in secret because they couldn't be together, it felt profoundly wrong to think about tearing it all down and erasing that history from...history. Turning this story into staged photos and granite countertops and a quick sale to the highest bidder may bring in enough money to pay her debts and escape her job, but at what price?

Ava looked down at her lap, and made a decision that she knew she may yet regret when back in her studio apartment, but for now it was the right choice. "I'll keep as much of the house as I can," she said.

Liam blinked. "Huh?"

She met his eyes, her jaw set with determination. "I'm not ripping it out. I'm keeping it exactly as it is. The pantry, the fireplace in the parlor, the window seats. If we can save it, we'll restore it. Whoever buys this house gets Beatrice and..."

"Thomas," he filled in

"Thomas' full vision of paradise."

Liam sat nodding, his face betraying a whir of thinking going on beneath, but Ava couldn't guess what was stirring deep in there. She pulled out her phone and pulled up her renovation notes. The neat, color-coded spreadsheet that had seemed so clear and logical a week ago now looked almost obscene in its efficiency. *Demo kitchen pantry - $800 savings. Remove fireplace surround - opens up floor plan. Replace window seat with standard window - more modern appeal.* She deleted each item methodically, one after another, watching her projected profit margin shrink with each tap.

"You don't have to," he said in his soft gravelly tones.

"I know." She looked up at him, and she knew her eyes were probably too bright, probably revealing too much. "But I want to. Debts be damned, eh? I need to... I can't... I can't erase them. Your grandfather and Beatrice. It feels wrong and I can't pretend it doesn't matter just because it's more profitable to ignore it."

Something shifted in Liam's expression. The last of the guardedness, the careful distance he'd maintained all week, crumbled away. What replaced it was so open, so genuinely warm, that Ava's breath caught in her throat, and that heat started growing in her chest again.

"Thank you," he said quietly.

They sat there in the golden afternoon light. The hole in the wall became a frame for the garden beyond, and Ava realized Liam had been right, there was something beautiful about the skeleton of the house. About seeing its bones, understanding how it held itself together. The light flowed differently now, reaching corners it had never touched before. The kitchen felt bigger, brighter, but also more honest somehow. Like the house was finally showing her its true self.

"We should probably clean this up," Ava said eventually, making to stand up. "The wall debris, I mean. And figure out if I've created a structural nightmare by knocking out that section."

"It'll be fine," Liam said, also standing, but with a groan betraying the effort it had taken to support the wall. "The beam above held, and I can brace that cracked post. And actually..." He gestured to the opening with his free hand. "It does open up the space. Makes it feel less claustrophobic. Your instinct wasn't wrong."

"Just my execution," Ava said wryly.

"Well, yeah, don't quit your day job to become a contractor." But there was no bite to the words, just gentle teasing.

Ava found herself smiling despite everything, despite the dust in her hair and the ache in her muscles and the way her careful business plan was unraveling in real-time, and the threat of having to work forever for Martin, living in her little box. She pushed that aside. "I'll leave the actual demolition to the professionals from now on. Promise."

"Probably for the best."

They fell quiet again, but it was a different kind of quiet than before. Comfortable. The kind of quiet that existed between people who had shared something important, something true. Finally, reluctantly, Ava began gathering the letters back into their packet. She handled each envelope with care, making sure they stayed in order, making sure the silk scarf was wrapped around the box just so. When she reached the last one, Liam's hand moved to help her, and their fingers brushed. It wasn't the first time they'd touched but this was different. Intentional. Liam's fingers lingered against hers, calloused and warm, but soft and gentle, as they both held the final envelope. Ava looked up and found him watching her with an expression she couldn't quite read. Soft and wondering, like he was seeing her for the first time. Like she'd surprised him.

"What?" she asked softly.

"Nothing." But he didn't look away. "Just... you're not what I expected."

"Neither are you."

His thumb traced across her knuckles again, that same unconscious gentleness. "No?"

"No." Ava's heart was beating too fast, her mouth dry. They were close now, closer than they'd been all week. His neck pulsed with each heart beat. It was as fast as hers. "I thought you were just a grumpy contractor who hated me."

"I never hated you." His voice was a growl, lower, and intimate in a way that made heat pool in Ava's stomach. "I just didn't understand you. Didn't understand why someone would want to change something that was already whole and then leave as soon as they arrived."

"And now?"

"Now, I think maybe you're not a heartless house-flipper after all."

"Just a house-flipper with a heart?" Ava meant it as a joke, but it came out too soft, too honest.

"Something like that."

The space between them almost sparkled, so charged it was with electricity. Ava was acutely aware of every point of contact. His hand in hers, their knees almost touching, the way his breath moved in his chest. This was dangerous, a rational part of her mind whispered. She was here to flip a house, make a profit, and get out. Get home. Getting involved with the contractor, getting *feelings* for the contractor, was the kind of mistake that derailed business plans and complicated everything. But...the tilt of his head, the way it highlighted his strong jaw. That smell of sawdust and pine and soap.

She opened her mouth to say something, what, she wasn't sure, but the sound of a truck engine made them both freeze and the spell was broken.

Liam pulled back first, releasing her hand. "That'll be Jake. I called him earlier to bring the dumpster for the demo debris."

"Right." Ava stood for a moment, trying to collect herself, trying to slow her racing heart. "Of course."

Liam stepped back, clearing his throat, his ears slightly red. "I'll, uh, I'll go deal with Jake. You should probably..." He gestured vaguely at her dust-covered clothes.

"Yeah. Probably." Ava looked down at her filthy jeans, top now more dust than cotton, arms streaked with grime. "I look like I've been through a war zone."

"You look like you've been doing actual work for the first time in your life," Liam said, and there was that teasing tone again.

"Thanks. I might go change into that yellow flannel. It'll hide the dirt well," she said.

"It'll look good on you." And before she could formulate a response to that, before she could parse whether he was flirting or just being friendly, he was gone, heading out the door to meet his friend.

The Storm and the Spark

The morning sky had traded its usual Oregon mist for a bruised, ominous palette of crimson and violet, a 'red sky in the morning' that looked less like a weather report and more like a warning. Ava left Liam working out in the garden, already so deep into the rhythmic *shave-shave-shave* of a hand plane that he hadn't even looked up when she'd announced her hardware run.

On her way back from Miller's, clutching a brown paper bag of high-end brushes, she stopped. On the porch of 'The Dust Jacket', a ginger tabby was sprawled across a stack of vintage crates, its belly rising and falling in a state of terminal coziness. The shop didn't just look inviting; it looked like a sanctuary. She realised she hadn't yet visited the store and it might stock some useful, if not dated, photo books with some inspiration for the bedroom layout she was toying with in her head. She could look it up online of course, but it would be rude to ignore such an inviting and friendly looking place when the opportunity was right in front of her. So she decided to head in.

As she pushed the heavy oak door open, a brass bell let out a muffled *thud-chimed*—the sound of a bell that had been rung so many times it had lost its sharp edge.

The smell hit her first. It wasn't the chemical "new book" scent of a Chicago megastore; it was the intoxicating aroma of vanilla, aged paper, and a faint, lingering hint of cinnamon tea. The air was noticeably heavier here, slowed down by the weight of ten thousand spines. Books didn't just line the walls, they colonized the floor in strategic, waist-high towers that looked like they might collapse if someone breathed too heavily in the direction of the "Classics" section. Hand-lettered signs hung from the rafters for a dizzying array of clubs: *The Tolkien Fellowship, The Mystery Mavens,* and something called *The Romance Rebels,* which featured a silhouette of a man who looked suspiciously like a muscular version of Silas.

"I promise they don't bite," a voice chirped from behind a literal fortress of leather-bound tomes.

A woman scrambled out, nearly toppling a stack of *National Geographics*. She was younger than Ava, with a halo of golden ringlets that seemed to be fighting a losing battle with a pair of oversized, thin-rimmed glasses.

"I'm Sophie," she said, practically vibrating with a friendly energy that made Ava feel suddenly very tired. Sophie brushed a cloud of white flour from her blouse, evidence of a mid-morning scone, and extended a hand that was warm and slightly dusty. "You're Ava. The Chicago Niece. The one with the power tools and the brave face."

Ava blinked, her 'city armor' momentarily chinked. "Is there a town-wide broadcast I missed? Does Silas have a radio show?"

Sophie laughed, a bright, melodic sound. "Worse. He has a stool at Mama's Diner. But don't worry, the consensus is that you're doing a 'God's work' sort of job on Aunt Bea's place. Most of us thought the rot would have claimed it by now."

"I'm trying to restore it, not just patch it," Ava found herself saying, surprised by the defensive pride in her own voice.

"I think it's great you're fixing up the cottage. Beatrice would've wanted it loved, not left to rot."

"Even if I'm selling it? I get the feeling that's not popular here."

Sophie shrugged. "Better sold than abandoned. And who knows? Maybe Willow Creek will grow on you."

Ava's defensive shoulders fell, just a little bit, melted by Sophie's genuine warmth and friendliness. "I was actually looking for something...

historical. For the bedroom," she said. "Not just a Pinterest board, but something with soul."

Sophie's eyes lit up behind her lenses, a spark of pure, librarian adrenaline. "Soul? Oh, we can do soul. Follow me. The Architecture section is behind the 'Local Poets' alcove, just past the cat's favorite sunspot."

For the next half hour, Ava was swept up in Sophie's wake. Sophie didn't just point to a shelf, she climbed a rolling ladder, pulled down heavy, cloth-bound volumes, and spoke about 'aesthetic integrity' with the fervor of a preacher. She was a force of nature, a woman who seemed to know exactly which page held the secret to a neo-Victorian molding.

When Ava finally emerged back into the red-tinted morning light, she was carrying three books, a flyer for an Art Club she was 90% sure she'd attend, and a strange, bubbling sense of belonging. In Chicago, a shop assistant was a hurdle to be cleared. Here, Sophie was a gateway.

Ava looked back at the shop one last time. For a woman who was supposed to be on a tight deadline, she was starting to collect a lot of reasons to walk a little slower.

Armed with her paintbrushes and inspiration, she headed back to the cottage ready to take on the cottage's next big challenge.

The sky had been threatening all afternoon, evolving from the red of the morning to the color of a fresh bruise, purple and yellow at the edges, then sickly green at its heart. Ava dabbed her brush against the window trim for what must have been the hundredth time, watching the paint refuse to cooperate, despite the new, top quality brush. It stayed tacky under her fingers, refusing to dry in the oppressive humidity that pressed against the cottage like a living thing.

"You're fighting a losing battle there."

She turned to find Liam standing in the doorway, toolkit in hand. His hair was darker with sweat, and there was a smudge of sawdust across his forearm that she absolutely should not be noticing.

"The paint won't stick," she said, frustrated. "It's like trying to ice a cake in a sauna."

"That's because a storm's coming." He nodded toward the window. "A bad one, by the looks of it. You need to batten down the hatches."

Ava glanced outside. The trees weren't just swaying anymore they were bowing, like supplicants before an angry god. The cheerful creek she'd grown fond of watching from her bedroom window had already swollen, its voice changing from a babble to something closer to a growl.

"How bad?" she asked, setting down her brush.

"Well, the creek's already risen. So, bad enough that I should get going before..."

The sky opened.

There was no preamble, no gentle patter building to a crescendo. One moment the world was holding its breath, and the next it was drowning. Rain didn't fall so much as attack, slamming against the cottage roof with a sound like a thousand drummers gone mad. The windows streamed instantly, turning the world outside into an impressionist painting of grays and greens. Liam swore and moved to the window. Ava joined him, and her stomach dropped.

In no time, the creek was no longer a creek. It was a river, brown and furious, clawing at its banks. The speed with which it had changed took Ava by surprise. The gravel driveway was instantly transformed into a churning stream of mud and debris.

"I need to move my truck," Liam said, already heading for the door.

"You can't go out in that!" Ava shouted to be heard above the rain.

"If I don't move it now, it could be buried in mud."

He was out the door before she could argue further. Ava pressed her face to the window, heart hammering as she watched his dark shape move through the deluge. The rain was so thick she could barely see him. When he reached the truck, he was ankle-deep in flowing mud running from the road and through her garden on an unstoppable march to the creek at the back. The engine started but the tires just spun. Mud sprayed up in rooster tails as Liam tried to reverse, to move forward, to do anything. The truck didn't budge. It sat there like a boulder. After an eternity passed in a few moments, he gave up. He ran back to the cottage, and Ava had the door open before he reached it. He stumbled inside, water streaming off him like he'd just climbed out of a pool.

"It's stuck," he said unnecessarily.

"Yes," said Ava, a little sarcastically.

He dragged a hand through his soaked hair. Water droplets flew everywhere. "The main road will be flooded by now given the state of that creek."

"So you're..." Ava's voice trailed off.

"Stuck." He met her eyes, and something unreadable flickered across his face. "Here. With you."

"Yes," she said again. Unsaid words hung in the air between them, heavy with implications neither of them was ready to name.

Then the lights went out.

The darkness was absolute, the kind of black that Chicago never knew. No streetlights bleeding through windows, no glow from neighboring buildings, no electronic devices casting their blue-white pallor. Just darkness, deep and complete, broken only by the occasional flash of lightning that threw the gutted rooms into sharp relief. Ava's breath caught. It wasn't the dark she feared, it was the silence underneath the roar of the rain. The sudden absence of the refrigerator's hum, the laptop's quiet whir, all the small mechanical sounds that had kept her company. Now there was just the storm, the crackle of the last bit of dying daylight through the clouds, and Liam's breathing somewhere to her left.

"Don't move," his voice came from the darkness. "Let me find the candles."

"You know where they are?" Ava heard her own voice, smaller than she wanted it to be.

"Beatrice had an emergency kit. She was prepared for everything." There was warmth in his tone when he spoke about her great-aunt, a fondness that made Ava's chest tighten. "Stay there. I'll be right back."

She heard him moving through the cottage with the confidence of someone who knew every creaking floorboard, every jutting corner...

"Ow!" Came a cry...but not where she left that sledgehammer though. Ava stayed frozen where she was, one hand pressed against the window frame, feeling strangely abandoned in the dark.

A match flared, and Liam's face appeared in the golden glow like a ghost made solid. He touched the match to a thick pillar candle, and the darkness retreated by a few inches. "Found them," he said, lighting another. And another. Soon he had five candles burning, their flames dancing in the drafts that found their way through the old cottage walls. The shadows they cast were huge and flickering, making the gutted rooms feel less like a construction site and more like... something else. Something secret and separate from the world. Ava found herself watching the way the light played across his face as he moved, highlighting the sharp line of his jaw, the curve of his mouth. He'd changed since that first morning, or maybe she was just finally starting to see him clearly.

"The stove is electric," Liam said, holding a candle up to survey the kitchen. "So no hot food."

"What do we have that's cold?"

They cobbled together a strange meal from the supplies Ava had: crackers and cheese, some slightly bruised apples, a bar of expensive dark chocolate she'd been saving. Liam found a bottle of red wine in Beatrice's pantry that was probably older than Ava.

"She wouldn't mind," he said, working the cork free with a pocketknife. "Beatrice believed wine was meant to be drunk, not collected."

"Why was she saving that one then?"

"I don't know. Psychic powers?"

Ava rolled her eyes, but couldn't help but smile.

They ended up in the living room, the only room with a working fireplace. Liam built a fire with the same efficient competence he brought to everything, and soon warmth began to push back against the cold that had crept in with the storm. The roof amplified every raindrop into a symphony of percussion, so loud they had to lean close to hear each other speak, which wasn't so bad as the temperature was starting to fall.

Ava sat on the floor with her back against the sofa, legs stretched toward the fire. Liam settled nearby, close enough that she could feel the heat radiating from him mixing with the heat from the flames. He'd stripped off his wet flannel shirt and sat in just a t-shirt that clung to his shoulders in a way that made Ava very focused on her wine glass.

"This is probably not how you imagined spending your evening," she said, taking a sip. The wine was rich and complex, tasting of cherries and earthy undertones.

"I've had worse." Liam accepted the bottle when she passed it to him. "And you?"

Ava thought about her Chicago evenings, the business dinners that lasted too long, the networking events where every conversation was a chess game, the nights alone in her apartment with takeout and her laptop, always working, always trying to prove something and get ahead.

"No," she admitted. "This is... different."

'Different' didn't cover it. She was sitting on the floor of a half-renovated cottage with a man who'd barely tolerated her a week ago, eating crackers by candlelight while a storm tried to tear the roof off. She should have been miserable. Anxious. Panicking. Desperate to get back to civilization. Instead, something she couldn't quite name, warm and settling like coming home after a long journey, settled upon her.

The fire crackled, sending up a shower of sparks. The smell of woodsmoke mixed with the damp cedar scent that permeated the cottage, creating an atmosphere both wild and comforting. Outside, the storm raged on, but inside this small circle of firelight, Ava was strangely safe and calm.

"Can I ask you something?" Liam's voice was quiet, nearly lost under the drumming rain.

"Sure."

"Why did you really leave Chicago?"

The question landed between them like a stone dropped in still water. Ava took another sip of wine, buying time, but the alcohol had loosened something in her chest. The thing she'd been holding so tightly for months, the hurt and humiliation she'd been trying to outrun.

"I came to do up this house and sell it, you know that."

"No, you could have done that with an agent. Or a short visit. You're an architect, you've done builds remotely I'm sure." Ava sipped the wine. "You took 30 days off work but are apparently desperate to get back." He took a beat. "Beatrice told me you were stuck. And you might need help. But that's for more than just construction work isn't it?"

She knew he had gambled by putting that out into the room. She should have responded sharply telling him to mind his own business. She should have told him Beatrice didn't know her, and Chicago is just perfect, thank you very much. But maybe it was the wine. Maybe it was the darkness outside the firelight, making confession feel safe. Maybe it was just that she was tired of carrying it alone.

"There was a man," she began, and Liam's expression shuttered slightly. "Martin. Senior partner at the firm. He was my mentor when I started, but it became... He was a brilliant strategist, everyone said. I was lucky to work under him." She laughed, but there was no humor in it. "He was...is...married. I didn't know at first, and when I found out, I ended it. Told him it was wrong, not to mention unprofessional, and that it was over." The words came faster now, like poison she needed to purge. "But Martin didn't like being told no. Eventually I reported directly to him, and I was worried it would be awkward but I told myself I was young and stupid and it was well over by that point and everything would be fine. It wasn't fine. Over time he started undermining me in meetings. Stealing my ideas and presenting them as his own. I've been an associate there for six years but I finally had a promotion coming. Creative Director. I'd been working towards it for ages. And then..."

"He took it," Liam said quietly.

"He didn't just take it, he gave it away to the most undeserving..." She trailed off. If she was telling the story, she was telling it all. "He spread rumors that I'd slept my way into consideration. Made me look incompetent and manipulative at the same time." Ava could feel her eyes burning, but she refused to cry. She'd cried enough over Martin Jones. "HR investigated me, not him. They cleared me, but the damage was done. Everyone looks at me differently now. Like I was either a victim or an opportunist, and neither version of me is someone anyone would want to work with."

"Why haven't you left?"

"I can't, I'm stuck. Martin has told too many important people I'm the scorned lover so I'd be starting again anywhere else, and I can't afford to go out alone. I have rent and bills and... Some days I feel barely above water on the amounts I owe in loans and hire purchase payments. Chicago is so expensive.

"I got the message about Aunt Bea and I knew this was my chance. I just need to get out ahead and regain control of my life. I feel...I feel like I haven't been in control of anything for so long. Going through motions and not living, you know? I can't stand the whispers, the sympathetic looks, the way people change the subject when I walk into a room." She traced a finger along the rim of her wine glass. "I'm building a new chance so when I get back I can break free and live again, not just exist."

The words hung in the candlelit air. Liam was quiet for a long moment, firelight playing across his features. When he finally spoke, his voice was rough.

"He's a coward."

"He's a senior partner at one of the biggest firms in Chicago."

"He's still a coward." Liam shifted, moving slightly closer. "Takes a special kind of weakness to destroy someone's career because they wounded your ego. You're better off away from him. Block his number, delete his details, never think of him again."

"I can't do that, I need that job. And I'm in the middle of nowhere, scraping paint off a house I didn't know existed a month ago."

"You can be free now," Liam said simply. "Free of him, free of people who'd believe his lies, free of a place that didn't deserve you." He paused. "You don't see it yet, but you will."

Ava looked at him, really looked. The firelight had found the golden flecks in his eyes again, but it was more than that. There was understanding in his expression, hard-won and genuine. This wasn't empty platitude. He meant it.

"How do you know?" she asked softly.

"Because I've been where you are." Liam took another drink. "Not the same situation, of course, but... I tried to leave Willow Creek once. Right after college. Had a job offer in Seattle. Big construction company, good money, the whole package. I thought I was supposed to want that. Thought that if I left this place then nothing else could leave me. I'd be free and living the good life, like staying in a small town meant giving up on ambition." He drank again.

"What happened?"

"I hated every minute of it." He laughed, shaking his head. "Hated the traffic, the noise, the way everyone moved so fast they forgot to see each other. Hated working on projects I didn't care about for clients who just wanted the cheapest option. I hated doing a job instead of crafting a solution, you know? I lasted eight months before I came back with my tail between my legs."

"That doesn't sound like failure," Ava said.

"Tell that to my mother. She had my whole life planned out, college, big city job, marriage to someone 'worthy of me.'" He made air quotes around the word. "Coming back to Willow Creek to work with my hands wasn't part of her vision. But I realised that this is where I belong. Where I can build things that matter, that last. Where I know my neighbors and they know me." Liam's voice softened. "Where I can take my time and do things right, instead of just doing them fast."

Ava thought about her Chicago life, the velocity of it, the constant motion that never quite got her where she wanted to go. She'd thought Martin and the partnership and the corner office were what she wanted. But maybe she'd just been running toward what she was supposed to want.

"I don't miss it," she said suddenly. "Chicago. I thought I would, thought I'd hate it here. But when I wake up and hear the creek instead of sirens, when I can see stars at night... I don't miss the noise. Or the glass towers. Or any of it."

The admission surprised her as much as it seemed to surprise Liam. They looked at each other across the firelight, the flickering light and crackling wood a homely accompaniment to the rain on the roof and whistling wind. Something shifted in her chest. A wall coming down, or maybe a door opening.

"You're not who I thought you were," Liam said quietly.

"Neither are you."

The rain continued its assault on the roof, so loud now that the world beyond their circle of firelight ceased to exist. There was only this room, this fire, this moment. Liam was close enough that Ava could see the pulse beating in his neck, could count the days of stubble on his jaw.

He reached out slowly, giving her time to move away. She didn't.

His hand came up to her face, thumb brushing across her cheekbone with a gentleness that made her breath catch. "You have paint," he whispered. "Right here."

His thumb moved in a slow circle, wiping away the smudge she must have transferred earlier. But the paint was gone and his hand was still there, cradling her cheek. His palm was rough, warm and solid, and Ava found herself leaning into the touch without meaning to. The air between them had gone thick and electric. Liam's eyes had darkened, his gaze dropping to her mouth and then back up, asking a question he didn't voice. Ava's heart was hammering so hard she was sure he could hear it over the rain.

He leaned in, just an inch. Then another. She could smell the wine on his breath mixing with woodsmoke and cedar. Her eyes started to drift closed—

ACHOO!

The sneeze was massive, wet, and accompanied by a full-body shake that sent droplets of water flying everywhere. Barnaby, who had been sleeping peacefully by the fire, had chosen that exact moment to wake up and express his opinion on being damp.

Ava jerked back, and Liam's hand fell away from her face. They stared at the dog, who looked back at them with that expression of blissful ignorance only dogs could manage.

"Barnaby," Liam said, somewhere between amused and exasperated. "Really?"

The dog yawned, showing all his teeth, then stretched out even closer to the fire, completely unconcerned with the moment he'd just destroyed.

Ava started laughing. She couldn't help it. The tension, the wine, the sheer absurdity of being interrupted by a sneezing dog. Liam joined her, and soon they were both shaking with it, the almost-kiss hanging in the air between them like something they'd revisit when they could breathe again.

"I should..." Liam gestured vaguely. "We should probably get some sleep. It's late."

"Right. Yes." Ava nodded too enthusiastically. "Sleep. That's... yes."

Ava moved to the base of the stairs, her candle flickering, going to head up to bed. Liam started to mess around with blankets and the sofa. Upstairs was her old life, privacy, boundaries, and cold sheets. Downstairs was the scent of cedar smoke, the steady sound of Liam's breathing, and a warmth that had nothing to do with the fire. She made a decision.

"The bedroom is going to be freezing," she said, unconvincingly. "And terribly loud, being so much closer to the roof with all this rain."

Liam hesitated, then continued with a small nod. "I know. Stay by the fire. I'm not going to bite."

They arranged their sleeping situation with the awkward formality of people trying very hard not to acknowledge what had almost happened. He grabbed some drop cloths from the renovation supplies and made himself a nest on the floor, close enough to tend the fire through the night but far enough from the sofa to be proper.

Ava lay in the darkness, listening to the rain and the crackle of the fire and Liam's breathing as it gradually deepened into sleep. She should have been uncomfortable, the sofa was lumpy and too short, and she could feel every spring. But wrapped in one of Beatrice's quilts, warm from the fire, she felt something she hadn't felt in months.

Safe.

Not the brittle, fragile safety of locked doors and alarm systems. Not the performative safety of corporate policies and HR departments. But real safety. The kind that came from being seen—truly seen—and not found wanting. She thought about Liam's hand on her face, the way he'd looked at her like she was something precious instead of damaged. She thought about his story of leaving and returning, of finding home in the place everyone else wanted to escape. She thought about her own admission, that she didn't miss Chicago, didn't miss the life she'd built there.

Outside, the storm raged on, but inside, Ava drifted toward sleep feeling like maybe, she'd finally stopped running. And maybe what she'd been running toward had been here all along, waiting in a cottage on a mountainside, in the hands of a man who built things that lasted. It was a scary thought, but a warm and inviting one at the same time. Lightning flashed, briefly illuminating the room. In that moment, she saw Liam's profile against the firelight, the strong line of his jaw, the sweep of his lashes against his cheek, one arm thrown over his head in sleep. He looked different than the grumpy contractor who'd glared at her that first morning. He looked like a protector.

Thunder rolled across the mountain, shaking the walls, and Ava closed her eyes. Tomorrow they would wake and likely rebuild their careful distance, and pretend the moment by the fire had never happened. Tomorrow the storm would pass and the flood waters would recede and Liam would find a way to unstick his truck and leave. But tonight, they were here together, listening to the rain and each other's breathing, two people who'd both run from the wrong things and might have finally found the right place to stop.

Ava pulled the quilt closer and let sleep take her, a smile playing at the corners of her mouth. The storm could rage. She was exactly where she needed to be.

One Step Forward...Two Steps Back

The morning arrived with the kind of clarity that only follows a storm. Ava woke to pale sunlight streaming through the cottage windows, turning the dust motes into dancing flecks of gold. For a moment, suspended between sleep and waking, she forgot about the lumpy sofa springs digging into her hip, forgot about her dwindling bank account, forgot about everything except the profound sense of rightness that had settled over her sometime during the night.

Then she heard it. The gentle hiss and bubble of something brewing, and underneath that, the crackle of a fire.

She sat up, her borrowed blanket pooling around her waist, and found Liam crouched by the fireplace, feeding kindling into flames that had already taken hold. He'd changed his shirt but was still wearing yesterday's jeans, and there was something unspeakably intimate about witnessing his morning routine, about being here in this space that was so completely his.

"You're awake," he said without turning around. "Good timing. Coffee's almost ready."

"Coffee?" Ava's voice came out rough with sleep. "Is the power back?"

"No." He stood, brushing bark dust from his hands, and crossed to the small kitchenette they'd set up where a battered stovetop percolator sat on a camping stove she hadn't noticed before. "Found this in the shed. My grandfather used to say that real coffee doesn't need electricity, just patience and respect for the process."

The aroma that filled the cottage was nothing like the efficient, sterile brew from her Chicago Starbucks. This was something earthier, richer, coffee that announced itself with authority. Ava pulled the blanket around her shoulders and padded over, her feet cold against the wooden floor.

"You didn't have to do all this," she said softly.

Liam glanced at her, and the look that passed between them carried the weight of last night, of lightning and confessions, of the moment when the world had narrowed to the space between their bodies. The Almost Moment, Ava thought..

"Seemed like the right thing to do." He poured coffee into two mismatched mugs, handing her one. Their fingers brushed in the transfer, and the touch went all the way to her bones. "Besides, we've got a big day ahead."

Right. Reality settled back over Ava's shoulders like a familiar coat. She had a house to flip, a timeline to meet, and a profit margin that was already looking shakier than she wanted to admit. Whatever had sparked between them last night would have to wait, or maybe, a small voice whispered, it would simply fade away once she went back home, back to her real life. The thought made her chest ache in a way she didn't want to examine too closely.

"Right. Ready to get to work?" she asked.

Liam's smile was slow, almost teasing. "With you, Gardiner? Always."

They were halfway through their makeshift lunch, sandwiches from Mama C's, when they heard the crunch of gravel in the driveway. Ava looked up to see a woman in her late sixties tottering down the drive, her perfectly coiffed white hair catching the afternoon sun, a covered pie dish balanced in her manicured hands.

"Oh no," Liam grumbled under his breath.

"What?"

"Mrs Gable. The town's unofficial, official information network." He stood, brushing crumbs from his jeans. "Brace yourself."

Mrs Gable approached with the purposeful stride of someone on a mission, her eyes already cataloging everything, the state of the house, the tools scattered across the porch, the way Ava and Liam had been sitting perhaps a touch closer than strictly professional.

"Liam McGregor!" she called out, her voice deep and commanding. "I heard you were working on the old Gardiner place. And you must be Ava Gardiner." She turned to Ava with a smile that was equal parts welcoming and assessing. "Beatrice's great-niece from Chicago. We've all been dying to meet you properly."

Ava stood, acutely aware of the dust covering her clothes, the paint flecks in her hair. "Mrs Gable I presume? It's nice to meet you."

"Oh, call me Eleanor, dear. Everyone does." She thrust the pie dish toward Ava. The tone of her voice and commanding presence told Ava that no one would ever dare call Mrs Gable 'Eleanor' to her face, not if they wanted to escape unharmed. Ava had met many people with that commanding presence and personality before and knew that asking people to call her 'Eleanor' was a polite formality everyone politely agreed to ignore. Some people are just meant to have a title, and Mrs Gable was one of them.

"I brought you a welcome pie," said Mrs Gable. "Apple crumble, my specialty. Silas mentioned you'd been working yourself ragged out here, and I thought, 'That poor girl needs some proper sustenance.'"

Ava accepted the still-warm dish, the sweet scent of cinnamon and brown sugar making her mouth water. Barnaby was instantly a lot more awake and interested in what was going on around him. "That's very kind of you. Thank you."

"Not at all, not at all." Mrs Gable's eyes swept over the house with barely concealed curiosity. "My goodness, you've made remarkable progress. Mama C said you'd taken to the work like a duck to water, and I can see she wasn't exaggerating. Those windows look absolutely transformed."

There was something slightly unsettling about the way Mrs Gable spoke, as if she'd been receiving regular updates on Ava's every move. Which, Ava was beginning to realize, she probably had been. "You've spoken to Mama C? About me?" Ava asked.

"Oh, of course dear. And she's been singing your praises all over town. Says you're not afraid of hard work, despite being from the city." Mrs Gable said 'the city' the way one might say 'the moon' a distant, slightly alien place. "She also mentioned you've got quite the eye for color. That sage green you chose for the shutters is just perfect."

Ava blinked. She'd only decided on the paint color yesterday, and they hadn't even started applying it yet. How did Mrs Gable know?

"Dale at the hardware store is quite pleased with your business," Mrs Gable continued, settling herself on the porch steps as if she'd been invited to stay. "He said you knew exactly what you needed. Very impressive for someone who'd never done renovation work before."

"I've been doing a lot of research," Ava said weakly.

"Oh, I'm sure. And Liam's been a wonderful teacher, I imagine." Mrs Gable's eyes sparkled with something that looked suspiciously like matchmaking glee. "He's quite talented, our Liam. Beatrice always said he had the best hands in three counties." She paused, letting that hang in the air for a beat too long. "For carpentry work, of course."

Liam's ears had gone distinctly pink. "Mrs Gable, I'm sure you have somewhere else to be..."

"Not particularly. I'm retired, dear. Time is something I have in abundance." She turned her attention back to Ava, her expression softening slightly. "Beatrice would be so pleased to see someone caring for her house properly. She loved this place more than anything. Well," she paused meaningfully, "almost anything."

There was a weight to those words, a hint of knowledge about Beatrice's secret past that made Ava's pulse quicken. "Did you know Beatrice well?" Ava asked.

"Well enough to know she had her secrets." Mrs Gable smiled, standing and brushing invisible dust from her pristine slacks. "But then, don't we all? Some of us are just better at keeping them than others." Her gaze flicked meaningfully between Ava and Liam. "Though in a town this size, very few secrets stay secret for long."

She started back toward the drive, then paused and turned. "Oh, and Ava dear? Welcome to Willow Creek. Officially. You're doing Beatrice proud, and that's no small thing."

As Mrs Gable tottered away to her own house down the street, Ava looked at the pie in her hands, then up at Liam, who was shaking his head with a rueful smile.

"How does she know everything?" Ava asked.

"It's a gift. Or a curse, depending on your perspective." He nodded toward the pie. "But her apple crumble really is exceptional, so there's that."

The master bedroom occupied the entire eastern side of the second floor, a sprawling space with high ceilings and three tall windows that would flood the room with morning light once Ava got around to replacing the heavy velvet curtains that currently blocked most of it. The wallpaper here was particularly egregious. A Victorian floral pattern in shades of burgundy and gold that might have been fashionable a century ago, was probably out of date when the house was built, and now just looked oppressive.

"This," Ava announced, running her hand along the textured surface, "has to go. I'm thinking a soft gray-blue for the walls. Something soothing. People buy houses with their imaginations, and this" she gestured at the wallpaper, "makes it impossible to imagine anything except living in your grandmother's house."

"Hey," Liam protested mildly, setting up the steamer. "My grandmother had excellent taste."

"Did she like burgundy florals?"

"Hmpph," he said, which Ava knew was as good a concession as she'd get.

They fell into an easy rhythm, Liam steaming sections of wallpaper while Ava followed behind with a scraper, peeling away layers of paper and paste that had been applied decades before. It was satisfying work, destructive but purposeful, each strip revealing a bit more of the original plaster beneath. Ava found herself stealing glances at Liam as they worked. There was something hypnotic about the way he moved, the controlled strength in his arms as he maneuvered the steamer, the focus in his expression. The clean line of his jaw. Ava had to force herself to concentrate on her scraper instead of on the flex of muscle under his shirt.

God, she had it bad.

They were making excellent progress, the room slowly emerging from beneath its dated shell, when they reached the far corner behind the old mahogany wardrobe. Liam had to shift the heavy piece away from the wall, and the moment he did, the smell hit them.

Musty. Damp. Organic decay.

"Oh no," Ava whispered.

The wallpaper here was different, darker, with visible water stains blooming across its surface. When Liam applied the steamer, the paper came away in wet, heavy chunks, and what it revealed made Ava's stomach drop to her feet.

Black mold. Not just a small patch, but a massive sprawling network that stretched from floor to ceiling, spreading like dark veins across the lath and plaster. It was furry in places, almost alive, with a texture that made Ava think of something that belonged in a horror movie rather than her renovation project.

"Don't touch it." Liam's voice was sharp as he grabbed her wrist, pulling her hand back before her scraper could make contact. "Ava, step back."

The command in his tone was so unlike his usual easy manner that Ava obeyed immediately, her heart hammering. "How bad is it?"

Liam's jaw tightened as he examined the wall, careful not to disturb the mold. "Bad. This is black mold. Probably from a leak in the roof or the plumbing. It's been growing behind this wallpaper for years, maybe decades."

"Can we just... scrape it off? Treat it?"

"Not really." He turned to face her, and the gravity in his expression made her chest constrict. "You know, this really requires a professional crew. The whole wall needs to come down, possibly more, depending on how far it's spread. They'll need to contain the area, use negative air pressure, remove all the affected materials, treat the remaining structure..." He trailed off, reading something in her face. "Ava, this could be expensive, and add weeks to your timeline."

Weeks.

Ava's mind was already doing the math, numbers cascading through her thoughts like a slot machine landing on bankrupt. A remediation company would charge thousands. Then the structural repairs, the replacement materials, the extended timeline eating into her already tight budget. Her thirty-day profit margin, the one she'd been counting on to finally give her an escape route, was evaporating like steam from Liam's wallpaper remover. She thought of the handbags she'd coveted but never bought, the shoes she'd admired in shop windows but walked past because she was trying to be responsible, trying to save every penny. Of this opportunity landing in her lap and giving her a way up and out. A future. And now the universe was cruelly ripping that away from her again, putting her back where she started. No, maybe worse than where she started. All of the sacrifice, the planning, the careful budgeting... It felt like a cosmic joke.

Her heart rate was picking up. Her breathing shallow.

"How much?" Her voice sounded strange, distant.

"If we do proper remediation? Three to five thousand, probably. Maybe more, depending on—"

"I don't have...I can't...I only have..." Ava's breath began to shorten, her heart rate started to climb as share began to spiral into shock. Then words started to tumble out brittle and sharp. "Total. Ruin. After the materials we've already ordered and my living expenses. Complete ruin."

Liam's eyes widened slightly, and somewhere Barnaby whimpered, but she couldn't stop now. The restriction in her throat had taken full effect. She had trouble breathing in because her lungs refused to breathe out. All her fears and desperation she'd been holding back were released at once and panic set in. The dam had broken, and everything came flooding out all at once.

"Do you know what it's like to spend six years at the same job, doing the same pointless work? Watching people who started after you get promoted while you're still sitting in the same cubicle making the same salary?" Her voice cracked, rising. "I've been going through the motions for so long I can't even remember what it feels like to care about anything I do. And I kept thinking, if I just work harder, if I just prove myself, they'll finally see me. They'll finally give me a chance. Then living with the gossip and humiliation of Martin and being kicked back down again. "

She was pacing now, her hands gesturing wildly, the scraper still clutched in one fist like a weapon. "When they posted that Director's position, I stayed late every night for three months writing the perfect application, putting together a portfolio of my work, practicing my interview until I could recite it in my sleep. And they gave it to Derek! Derek, who spends half his day watching football highlights and the other half taking credit for other people's ideas."

The words tasted like ash in her mouth. "So I smiled and congratulated him and went back to my desk and realized that I was never getting out. That this was my life forever. Waking up at six-thirty to catch the 'L' Train, sitting under fluorescent lights until my eyes burned, going home to a studio alone and doing it all again the next day. For forty more years."

Her voice broke completely now, all her fears and inner struggles were coming out with tears she'd been holding back for months. "When Great Aunt Bea left me this house, it was like...like the universe was finally throwing me a lifeline, you know? A chance to do something different. If I could flip this house, make enough profit, I could quit that soul-crushing job, clear the chains of debt around my neck and get away from that slime Martin. Actually figure out what I want to do with my life. I could have time to breathe, to think, to be something other than a cog in a machine that doesn't even notice I exist."

She turned to face the mold-ravaged wall, her chest heaving. "If this house fails, I'm not just back where I started. I'm worse. Deeper in debt, older, more desperate. I'll be stuck in that job forever, watching my life slip away one meaningless day at a time, knowing I had one chance to escape and I blew it on a house full of rot."

The silence that followed was broken only by her sobs. It was all out there now. No more secrets or lying to herself or Liam. She was defenseless. She couldn't bring herself to look at Liam, couldn't bear to see pity or judgment or worse, that careful professional neutrality contractors adopted when clients lost it. She expected him to say something meaningless and comforting. "It'll be fine." "We'll figure it out." "Every renovation has setbacks." The kind of platitudes that meant nothing, that were just words to fill the space until the crazy lady calmed down.

Instead, she heard his footsteps cross the room, and heard the sound of him rummaging in his tool bag. When he appeared in front of her, he was holding a respirator mask and a pair of heavy-duty gloves. "Here," he said simply.

Ava stared at the protective gear, confused. "What?"

"We don't fix it by crying." His voice was steady, matter-of-fact. "We fix it by stripping it to the studs."

Something in her chest shifted at those words. Not pity. Not false reassurance. Just acknowledgment of the problem and a clear path forward. He was treating her like an equal partner in the struggle, not a boss to be managed or a client to be placated. She took the mask and gloves with shaking hands.

"First," Liam continued, pulling on his own protective gear with practiced efficiency, "we seal off this room. Plastic sheeting, duct tape, the works. Then we very carefully remove the obviously compromised sections and bag them. That's not the full remediation, we'll still need that, but it'll reduce the spore count in the air and give us a better sense of the scope."

"You said it needs a professional?"

"Yeah, it ought to be done by a professional. But, it's not essential. I know what to do, and we can do it. Together." He adjusted his mask, his eyes meeting hers over the top of it. "This house is a fighter, Ava. It's survived a hundred and twenty years of storms and neglect and people who didn't see its worth. It's not going to let a little mold take it down. And neither are you."

The comparison should have been cheesy, but instead it steadied something inside her. She pulled on the gloves, the thick material awkward on her hands, and fitted the respirator over her face. When she looked at Liam, both of them now masked, armored against the toxic elements trying to destroy this house, she tried to resist an absurd urge to laugh.

"We look like we're about to rob a bank," she said, her voice muffled by the mask.

"Or perform surgery." He handed her a utility knife. "Dr. Gardiner. It's time to operate."

They worked for hours, moving with careful precision. Liam taught her how to score the wallpaper and plaster without releasing too many spores, how to bag the contaminated materials properly, and how to identify where the water damage originated. It was meticulous, exhausting work, and by the time they'd removed all the obviously affected sections, Ava's arms ached and her back screamed in protest. But there was something cleansing about it too. Each piece of rotted plaster they removed was a problem identified, a step toward solution. The room looked worse now, raw studs exposed, the scope of the damage fully visible, but it was an honest kind of ugliness. No more hiding behind pretty wallpaper. No more pretending the problems didn't exist.

When they finally pulled off their masks and stepped outside for air, the afternoon sun was already starting its descent toward the mountains.

"Come on," Liam said, stripping off his gloves. "We need to let the room air out, and you need to not look at this house for a few hours."

"Liam, I'm sorry I..."

"That's not a suggestion, Gardiner." But his tone was gentle. "Trust me on this. When you're drowning in the details, sometimes the best thing you can do is get some distance."

He drove them away from Bea's cottage, away from town, up a narrow road that climbed into the hills. Ava didn't ask where they were going, just leaned her head against the window and tried not to think what an idiot she'd been having a panic attack, losing her composure and spilling all her inner worries and thoughts to a man that she, really, barely knew. She watched the landscape change from manicured gardens to wild forest, the houses growing fewer and farther between until they disappeared entirely. Finally, Liam turned onto an unmarked dirt track that looked like it might be someone's driveway, or might just be a deer track. The truck bumped along for another quarter mile before emerging into a small clearing beside the creek.

"My spot," Liam said simply, killing the engine.

The creek was maybe twenty feet across. The sound of it was immediately soothing, that constant, musical burble that spoke of endless movement, of water that couldn't be stopped or contained, only redirected. Massive oaks leaned over the banks, their branches creating a cathedral-like canopy that filtered the sunlight into dappled patterns on the water. Liam led her to a fallen log that made a natural bench a few feet from the bank. The bark was worn smooth from use, his use, Ava realized. This was where he came when he needed to think, to escape, to remember who he was beneath all the professional competence and quiet strength. They sat in silence for a while, shoulder to shoulder, listening to the water. The tension of the day began to slowly drain out of her, replaced by a bone-deep weariness that wasn't entirely unpleasant.

"Oaks, not willows?" she asked finally.

"The large weeping willows in town were planted by the founders. They aren't native to the forest, though they do look good along the creek. I guess Willow Creek was an attempt to bring something from home. Try and control this place as part of founding a new town. There are willows here though," he said pointing to a row of bushes. "See that line of shrubs all along the waters edge, with the silvery green leaves? That's willow. Native to this area."

Now Ava saw them she realised she had seen those Willows throughout the town and all over her garden. She took joy now in knowing these were the native willows of Willow Creek.

"I used to come here with my grandfather," Liam said. "When I was a kid. He'd bring his fishing rod, and I'd bring a book, and we'd spend whole Saturdays here. Not talking much. Just... being."

Ava glanced at him. His profile was sharp against the dappled light, but there was a softness in his expression she had only seen glimpses of before. Vulnerability, she thought. The mask slipping away to reveal the man underneath.

"He taught me to see the mountains differently," Liam continued. "City people, no offense, they see them as permanent. Unchanging. But they're not. They're constantly breaking down and building up. Erosion and growth, decay and renewal, all happening at once. A forest fire you see as destruction? In five years, it'll be a meadow full of wildflowers that wouldn't have bloomed otherwise. That landslide that blocks the road? It's creating new soil, new habitats." He picked up a smooth stone from beside the log, turning it over in his hands. "Things have to break down to grow back stronger. The mountains know that. They've been doing it for millions of years."

Ava watched him, something warm and frightening unfurling in her chest. "Is this the part where you tell me mold is like a forest fire? Clearing the way for something better?"

"Maybe." His mouth quivered in a half-smile. "Or maybe I'm just trying to distract you from spiraling into financial panic by getting philosophical about geology."

"Is it working?"

"I don't know. Is it?"

The honest answer was yes, but not for the reasons he might think. It wasn't the metaphor about mountains or the soothing sound of the creek. It was him. The steadiness of his presence, the way he'd handed her tools instead of sympathy, the way he treated her problems as solvable rather than catastrophic. The way he made her feel like she wasn't alone in this, even though she barely knew him. Even though he was just the contractor she'd hired. Even though in a few weeks, assuming the house didn't bankrupt her first, she'd be back in Chicago and he'd be here, and this would all be just a strange interlude in both their lives.

Except it didn't feel like an interlude. This was something that mattered.

"Liam," she started, not sure what she was going to say, only knowing that she needed to say something, to acknowledge what was happening between them.

But before she could form the words, he turned to face her fully, and the look in his eyes stole her breath. It wasn't the careful, professional distance he usually maintained, it was the vulnerability of the night before. "The house will survive this," he said quietly. "And you will too. The question is, what do you really want when it's done?"

The question hung in the air between them, complicated and vital. Because he wasn't just talking about the house anymore. He was talking about her, about the choice she'd been avoiding since the moment she'd inherited the house. The choice between playing it safe, to sell the house, go back to Chicago and rescue her old life, or believing that something worthwhile might be waiting and possible here in Willow Creek.

The creek gurgled on, indifferent to human drama, following the only path it knew: forward, shaping itself around obstacles instead of being stopped by them.

"I don't want to leave," Ava heard herself say. The words came out soft but certain, surprising her with their truth. "Not yet. Not until I've seen what…might be possible…what the house can become."

Not until I've figured out what we can become, she didn't add. But she saw the understanding in Liam's eyes, the way his hand moved slightly toward hers on the log before stopping, hovering in the space between them.

"Then we'll make sure you don't have to," he said.

It wasn't a promise, exactly. It was something better, a declaration of intent, a commitment to stand beside her in the fight. They sat there until the shadows grew long and the afternoon grew old, two people in the wilderness, holding onto the fragile hope that sometimes, broken things were worth saving.

Roadtrip

The problem with black mold, Ava discovered, wasn't just that it existed. It was that killing it required chemicals with names she couldn't pronounce and equipment that apparently didn't exist in Willow Creek.

"Miller's Hardware doesn't carry industrial remediation supplies," Liam said, scrolling through his phone as they stood in her kitchen the next morning. "We'll have to go to Greenfield."

"Greenfield?" Ava wrapped her hands around her coffee mug, trying to ignore how he held his tongue while in deep thought looking at his phone.

"Two towns over. They've got a contractor supply store." He pocketed his phone and grabbed his keys from the counter. "My truck's the only thing that'll fit the dehumidifier and the air scrubber we need."

"Oooh. Roadtrip" she said.

Twenty minutes later, Ava found herself climbing into the passenger seat of Liam's truck, acutely aware that this was different from any hardware store run into town. This was a forty-minute drive each way. The cab was smaller than she'd expected. Or maybe Liam was just larger than her brain wanted to acknowledge. The space smelled of pine and old leather, with an underlying scent of sawdust that she associated strongly with him. His coffee, black, no sugar, sat in the cupholder between them, and when he reached for it, his forearm brushed against her knee.

"Sorry," he muttered, though he didn't sound particularly apologetic.

Ava shifted closer to the door, watching the familiar streets of Willow Creek give way to winding mountain roads. The morning was crystalline, the kind of autumn day where every leaf seemed to glow with its own inner light.

"You don't have to come, you know," Liam said, breaking the silence. "I know what we need."

"And miss the chance to see what passes for a 'big city' around here?" She kept her tone light, but the truth was more complicated. She wanted to come. Wanted to see how he navigated the world beyond Willow Creek. Wanted to understand the man who seemed to fill every space he occupied with quiet competence.

His mouth quirked. "It's got a Home Depot and a Walmart. Don't get too excited."

They fell into a comfortable silence, and Ava found herself relaxing into it. She'd spent so many years filling quiet spaces with small talk, with the kind of polite conversation that said nothing and meant less. But this was different. Natural. Like they'd already said everything that needed saying and could simply exist together.

When Liam shifted gears, his knuckles brushed her knee again. This time, neither of them apologized.

The "Greenfield Contractor Supply and Home Center" was exactly what it sounded like, a massive warehouse that smelled of lumber and possibilities. Something loosened in her chest as they walked through the automatic doors. This, at least, felt more like familiar territory. Not a small town hardware store, a big...well biggish...supplier. And she was used to dealing with suppliers.

"We need an industrial air scrubber, HEPA-rated," she told Liam, pulling out her phone where she'd made notes. "And the antimicrobial solution has to be EPA-registered for Class III mold remediation."

Liam raised an eyebrow, clearly impressed. "You've been doing homework."

She scanned the aisle markers. "Commercial equipment should be in the back."

She started walking, her boots clicking against the concrete floor with the kind of purposeful stride that came from years of navigating corporate offices. She could feel Liam following, and something about having him at her back made her stand a little straighter.

The commercial section was staffed by a middle-aged man with an impressive beard and a name tag that read "Dave—Manager."

"Help you folks?" he asked, looking up from his clipboard.

Ava shifted into what her assistant used to call her "Executive Voice", the one that could make board members sit up and pay attention. "I need a commercial air scrubber capable of handling 1,500 square feet, with true HEPA filtration. And I'll need a negative air machine if you have one in stock."

Dave's eyebrows climbed toward his receding hairline. "You doing professional remediation?"

"Personal project," Ava said smoothly. "I'll also need five gallons of your best antimicrobial concentrate. The spec sheet needs to show efficacy against Stachybotrys chartarum."

Behind her, she heard Liam make a sound that might have been a cough or a laugh.

Dave pulled out his tablet, fingers flying. "We've got the Phoenix Guardian, that's your top-of-the-line air scrubber. Runs about twelve hundred, but—"

"But you've got last year's model on clearance in the back for eight-fifty," Ava finished. She'd spent enough time negotiating vendor contracts to recognize the setup. "I'll take that one. And I noticed you're running a promotion on bulk chemical purchases."

Dave's grin was reluctant but genuine. "You're good. Yeah, buy four gallons, get the fifth at half price."

"I'll take five at the bulk rate, and you throw in the replacement HEPA filters." Ava smiled, the kind of smile that had closed million-dollar deals. "I'll be doing quarterly maintenance, so you're looking at a repeat customer."

"Deal." Dave shook his head, already typing. "Your husband's a lucky man."

Heat flooded her cheeks. "Oh, we're..."

"Business partners," Liam cut in smoothly, stepping up beside her. His hand settled briefly on the small of her back, a touch so light she might have imagined it. "She's the brains. I'm just the muscle."

Dave chuckled. "Whatever you say. Let me get this pulled for you."

As he walked away, Ava turned to Liam. "You didn't correct him."

"Didn't I?" His expression was unreadable, but something in his eyes made her pulse quicken. "Was I supposed to explain that you hired me to fix your dead aunt's cottage?" Liam crossed his arms, and Ava tried not to notice how the fabric of his flannel pulled across his chest. "That seemed like a long conversation."

It was a reasonable explanation. So why did her heart insist on doing complicated things in her chest?

While they waited for Dave to bring out the equipment, they wandered through the aisles. This wasn't like the cramped, dusty hardware store in Willow Creek. This was her kind of place, organized, efficient, with clear labeling and logical product placement. Liam found the tool section, examining a set of drill bits with the kind of focus most men reserved for sports cars or designer watches, or that children have with toys. She couldn't help but smile at his enthusiasm, and realized she liked seeing him unguarded, without the usual walls. For all his brawn and bluster, he had a capacity for wonder that he usually kept under lock and key. Watching that massive frame huddle over his new found toys with such focus made her smile. It was the most human thing she'd seen since she met him.

They loaded the equipment into the truck bed, or rather, Liam loaded it while Ava supervised and tried not to notice the flex of muscle beneath his shirt. Dave had thrown in the HEPA filters and knocked another fifty dollars off the total, which Ava considered a personal victory.

"You're dangerous in a negotiation," Liam observed as they pulled back onto the highway.

"It's all about knowing what the other person wants," Ava said. "Dave wanted to move old inventory and secure a repeat customer. I wanted quality equipment at a fair price. Everybody wins."

"Is that how you made business deals in your old life?"

His phrasing made her smile. "My 'old life' a few weeks ago."

"Yeah, but you're different now." He glanced over, then back at the road. "You stand different. Talk different. You're more..."

"More what?"

"Real," he said appreciatively.

The word hit her harder than it should have. Because he was right, she did feel more real here, in this small mountain town where nobody knew about her life or (stalled) career. Here, she was just Ava. And that was enough.

They were halfway back to Willow Creek when Liam pulled off at a roadside diner called "Rusty's Burgers and More." The "More" was apparently optimistic, from the outside, it looked like the kind of place that served exactly two things: burgers and fries.

"We should eat," Liam said, killing the engine. "It's past one."

Ava's stomach, right on cue, growled its agreement.

Inside, Rusty's was exactly what she expected, vinyl booths, a jukebox in the corner, and the smell of grease that was somehow comforting rather than off-putting. A waitress with "Marge" embroidered on her uniform waved them toward a booth by the window.

"What'll it be?" Marge asked, not bothering with menus.

"Two burgers, two orders of fries," Liam said. "And whatever pie you've got."

Ava raised an eyebrow. "You're ordering for me now?"

"You want something different?"

She considered it. "No. That sounds perfect." She smiled.

Marge grinned. "Young love. Ain't it sweet?" She gave a half hearted smile and bustled off before either of them could correct her.

"Does everyone in a fifty-mile radius think we're together?" Ava asked, bemused.

Liam leaned back against the booth, and the afternoon light streaming through the window turned his eyes almost golden. "Probably, but at least this isn't the gossip mill of Willow Creek so...it's not so terrible."

Her breath caught. Not so terrible? His previous reaction to being thought of as together had been to call her a stray and flighty...well, actually his previous reaction was "business partner" but now. Now it's "not so terrible". Is that a sign of progress? Is there some tacit indication that maybe he would be interested in...in exploring that Almost Moment from the other night? Or is he literally just saying that people thinking that isn't so terrible, but the actual idea itself is still terrible? Was she misreading his softening and opening up, is she over thinking these signs of kindness and the touches, and the creek and the drive...

But all she managed to say was: "No. Not so terrible."

The burgers arrived, massive, messy, perfect. They ate in companionable silence for a few minutes before Ava worked up the courage to ask the question that had been nagging at her.

"Why were you so concerned when you thought Silas would start to spread gossip about the two of us, that night he dropped off the casserole?"

Liam wiped his hands on a napkin, taking his time with the answer. He took a deep breath and let it out slowly. "My dad left when I was four. I only had my mom growing up. Most of the extended family was older, so by the time I was 15 I had attended more funerals than any other family celebration. Funerals seem to be the only time we came together to be honest. And 19 was when I lost Granddad Thomas who I was very close to. It was also when my high school girlfriend, and as of then the love of my life, left me for the bright lights of a big city."

"Oh, is that why you hate city girls so much?"

"No, it's why I hate people leaving so much. But" he conceded, "maybe I do lump all women from the city in that same bag as her. I look back and my main memory is that everyone I love leaves. Not always by choice, but they will eventually. As I got older, I've become more guarded about letting people into my life who are just going to leave without a hesitation or care. I don't want to deal with being let down like that, I don't want my friends and remaining family to be let down like that. I love Willow Creek, and Mama C, and Silas. Sometimes even Mrs Gable." He smiled. "And I don't want them trying to connect me with random women who don't stay around. Because I don't want to deal with the loss when they inevitably leave, and I don't want to see the disappointment on their faces when it doesn't work out."

"Isn't it lonely, sometimes? Don't you think that maybe some things are worth trying to see if, just maybe, they are better than lonely?"

"Yeah, it's lonely sometimes." He reached across the table for another napkin, and his fingers brushed hers where they rested near her water glass. "When someone comes along who wants to stay and be part of my life, and part of Willow Creek, maybe then I'll let them in. They've got to want to stay." He looked at her, as if asking a question but too afraid to put it into words.

Ava's heart was doing acrobatics in her chest. She should remember that she was leaving in a few weeks, that this was temporary, that Liam McGregor was her contractor and nothing more. That staying in a small town like this was not something she'd ever considered. That being connected to people, really connected in a way that they knew your business and knew...you...scared the life out of her. She'd be so vulnerable. So defenceless. In Chicago she'd be eaten alive if people knew her that well. She had been! By Martin, and that was just a rumour, not even the real her. She had to have defences, she couldn't let people in. Could she? Even in a town as small, and warm, and cozy as Willow Creek?

Liam seemed to read her mind and see she was struggling. He changed the subject.

"Tell me about Beatrice," he said. "Not the letters or the cottage, the Beatrice you knew. Tell me about her."

The question surprised her. No one had asked her about Aunt Bea, as they all seemed to know her better than Ava did. "She was magic," she said quietly. "When I was little, she would come visit for a few weeks every summer, and again near Christmas. Some years she'd drive. It's like a three, maybe four day road trip and Bea would turn up in this ridiculous old Cadillac, and we'd go out driving with all the windows down, singing along to Patsy Cline."

Liam smiled. "I remember that car. Bright red."

"The reddest red you've ever seen." The memories washed over her, bittersweet and achingly clear. "We'd spend the days doing everything from museums to picnics in the park. At night, she'd make cocoa, the real kind, with milk and chocolate chips melted in, and we'd sit in our garden and make up stories about the stars. She always had the best stories, and each of them had a moral or lesson she would expect me to work out before I was allowed another one."

"Sounds perfect."

"It was." Ava blinked hard against the sudden sting of tears. "I stopped being around for visits when I was sixteen. Got too busy with school, then college, then work. And I saw her less and less. And she got older and came less and less... I always meant to visit here, but there was always something else. Another deadline, another project."

"She understood," Liam said gently.

"Did she?" Ava looked up at him. "Because I'm not sure I do."

A moment passed between them. Then Ava said "tell me about the Beatrice you knew."

"She was great," chuckled Liam. "After I came back from Seattle, she really took me under her wing. There was always something that needed work in the house, and I was grateful for it, you know, having come back with practically nothing but grandad's tools to start a business with. I remember, one day, working in the garden digging out a drain. She was admiring the giant Weeping Willow at the back of the garden, and I was knee deep in thick, grey clay. She said 'isn't it the most beautiful thing in the garden' and I replied 'it's a thirsty invasive parasite with a good publicist.'"

Ava laughed.

"Yeah, she laughed too," said Liam. "'Willows have a GPS for old clay pipes, and this one is the reason your kitchen sink won't drain' I told her. 'Well sometimes a little inconvenience is the price you pay for nice things' she said." He adjusted his water glass, lost in the memory, smiling to himself. "She spent time telling me about my grandfather. She spent time helping me to get past the ones I'd lost, or had left me behind. She was there when I needed and helped me find myself and my place in Willow Creek.

"Before she got sick, we would talk about her plans for the house, when I'd stop repairing and start renovating. Her hopes and dreams for it, and whoever owned it next. But we never got there."

Ava nodded in silence. Beatrice had been married but never had children of her own, her husband dying relatively young. But she had had so much love to give, to Ava, and apparently to Liam, and no doubt many others in town. She was happy that she had decided to keep so much of the house and the spirit of Beatrice in it.

The jukebox, which had been playing upbeat country, suddenly switched to something slower. The opening notes of Patsy Cline singing "Crazy" floated through the diner. Ava's breath caught. "This was her favorite song."

"I know," Liam said softly.

They didn't dance. There was no room in the narrow booth, and besides, this moment was far too fragile for movement. Instead, they sat there, eyes locked, while Patsy sang about being crazy for loving someone.

When the song ended, Liam reluctantly said "We should get going. Sun'll set early, and I want to get that air scrubber installed before dark."

Ava nodded.

They split the bill, she insisted, he let her, and walked back to the truck. The afternoon had turned golden, that particular autumn light that made everything look like a photograph. As Liam opened her door, Ava noticed Marge watching them through the diner window, a knowing smile on her face. Let her think what she wants, Ava decided. It wasn't as if she could explain the truth when she didn't understand it herself.

The drive back to Willow Creek passed too quickly. They talked about small things, the best hiking trails, the worst movies they'd ever seen, whether pineapple belonged on pizza (Ava was firmly pro, Liam was horrified). But underneath the easy conversation, the weight of everything unsaid pressed down on her. This wasn't supposed to happen. Liam was her contractor. She was leaving soon. This was temporary. So why did temporary feel like the saddest word in the English language?

When they pulled into the cottage driveway, the sun was painting the sky in shades of amber and rose. The little house looked almost magical in the dying light, like something from a fairy tale. And standing by her mailbox, making absolutely no pretense of doing anything other than watching them arrive, was Mrs Gable.

"Evening, Liam," the older woman called, her eyes bright with interest. "Ava."

"Mrs Gable," Ava said weakly.

"My goodness, you two have been gone all day. Big shopping trip?"

"Had to go to Greenfield for supplies," Liam said, already moving to the truck bed. "Black mold remediation equipment."

"Oh, how industrious." Mrs Gable's smile was absolutely shameless. "I'll let you get to it. Just wanted to make sure everything was all right. You know how people talk."

"Oh, I'm sure they do," Ava said with a sigh.

Mrs Gable laughed, a sound of pure delight, and headed back toward her house. Ava could practically hear the phone calls already beginning: Did you see Ava and Liam come back from their day trip?

"She's going to tell everyone we were on a date," Ava said.

"Yep" Liam said resignedly. But it didn't have the level of intensity or panic of when Silas had left the casserole.

Had something shifted in Liam that being linked to Ava was no longer the worst thing in the world?

He set the scrubber down on the porch and turned to face her, and the way he was looking at her made all her carefully constructed arguments for and against being linked together (including, staying in Willow Creek) dissolve like sugar in rain.

"Help me down?" she managed to ask, suddenly aware that she was still standing on the high running board of his truck.

Liam moved closer, and Ava's breath shortened. His hands settled on her waist, strong and sure, and he lifted her down as if she weighed nothing at all. But instead of releasing her immediately, his hands lingered. His thumbs brushed against the skin just above her jeans, where her shirt had ridden up slightly. She realised it was the first time he'd touched her, not an arm or a knee, and she was all encompassed in his large grip. Strong, but gentle.

"You did good today, Gardiner," he said, his voice low and rough.

Something in his tone, the approval, the respect, the hint of something more, made her feel like she'd won a prize she hadn't known she was competing for.

"The 'City Girl' label," she whispered. "Is it officially gone?"

His mouth curved into that rare, devastating smile. "Yeah. It's gone."

For a moment, she thought he might kiss her. For a moment, she wanted him with an intensity that should have frightened her. She froze, her heart hammering. His gaze dropped to her mouth, then back up, and she saw the same want reflected there that was currently making her breath shallow. He leaned in. She didn't pull away. But in the instant where there could have been magic, there was Barnaby, nuzzling between them to say hello.

He stepped back, his hands sliding away from her waist, leaving cold spots where warmth had been.

"Let's get this equipment inside," he said. "Daylight's burning."

Ava nodded, not trusting herself to speak. *Is he interested or not?!* said her inner voice.

As she followed him toward the cottage, she caught a glimpse of movement in Mrs Gable's window down the road, the older woman pulling back a curtain, satisfaction written all over her face.

The Grain and the Ghost

"Hey, stranger!" Maya's text began. "I've been staring at my phone for days. Details. Now. How was the 'definitely-not-a-date' with Flannel God? Did you survive the rugged wilderness or did he finally break that corporate exterior?"

"It was fine, Maya." Ava wrote back. "We just went to Greenfields for supplies, some food on the way back. It was functional. He showed me the 'lay of the land.'"

"I bet he did!!! 'Lay of the land' Is that what the kids are calling it now??? Come on, Ava. I know your professiona' tone. You're holding out on me. Did he look at you with those brooding mountain eyes? Did you hold hands over the ketchup bottle?"

"Stop! It wasn't like that. But... if I'm being honest, it was actually nice. Comfortable, even. He didn't talk about ROI once. He actually knows the name of every tree. It was peaceful."

"Ha ha. Enjoy the mountain air while it lasts! Only a week and you'll be back on Dearborn with a real macchiato in your hand. You can tell me everything over mimosas. I've already got our Sunday brunch booked."

"Right. Can't wait."

Ava stared at the screen until the backlight dimmed. A sharp, unexpected pang tightened in her stomach at the mention of the brunch, a familiar ritual that was suddenly like a heavy coat she didn't want to put back on. Back on Dearborn. Macchiato. The thought of not drinking Mama C's coffee made her lip quiver.

She shook it off, tossed the phone onto the sawdust-covered duvet, and reached for her sanding block. She had a floor to finish.

The house had fallen into that particular kind of silence that only came after midnight, thick and velvet, broken only by the rhythmic *shhh-shhh* of sandpaper against wood. Ava's knees ached where they pressed against the drop cloth, and sweat had glued her yellow flannel to the small of her back, but she couldn't stop. Not now. Not when the hallway was finally revealing its secrets.

"Look at this," she breathed, sitting back on her heels and pushing damp hair from her forehead. "Is that—?"

"Quartersawn oak." Liam's voice came from behind her, roughened by hours of dust and minimal conversation. "Original to the house. See the ray fleck pattern?"

Ava leaned closer to where her sanding block had stripped away decades of grime and varnish. The wood beneath glowed honey-gold in the harsh light of the work lamps, its grain creating rippling patterns like water frozen mid-movement. Beautiful. Absolutely beautiful.

"I can't believe someone covered this with linoleum," she murmured.

"People do a lot of things in the name of modernization. Or profit" There was something in Liam's tone that made her glance back at him with a look. He was watching her with an expression she couldn't quite read, his face half-shadowed, dust settling in his dark hair like premature gray.

The air between them sparked, heavy with more than just sawdust. Ava turned back to the floor, pressing her sanding block down with renewed focus. *Shhh-shhh. Shhh-shhh.* The sound became meditative, a rhythm that matched her heartbeat. They'd been at this for three hours now, working in a companionable silence that was different from the tense quiet of their earlier weeks together. This silence was warm, punctuated by the occasional grunt of effort or satisfied hum when a particularly stubborn patch of finish finally yielded. The hallway was narrow, barely wide enough for them to work side by side, and every movement required careful choreography.

"Left," Liam said, and Ava shifted her weight to give him room to get past and reach the corner they'd been avoiding. His shoulder brushed hers as he moved past, and the contact was a spark in the darkness.

"Sorry," she murmured, though neither of them had done anything wrong.

"Don't be." His voice was low, almost lost in the sound of his sandpaper finding purchase on the wood. "Can't restore a floor without getting close."

Is he talking about the floor? Or something else entirely? Must be a sign! She pushed that voice back into its cupboard and went back to the floor.

The heat in the hallway was oppressive despite the cool night outside. They'd opened every window they could, but the work lamps threw off warmth that gathered in the narrow space like a fog. Ava could feel sweat trickling down her spine, gathering at her temples, making her clothes cling uncomfortably. She probably looked like a disaster, red-faced and grimy, her hair escaping its ponytail in wild curls. But when she glanced at Liam, she found him looking at her with something that definitely wasn't disgust.

He looked away quickly, focusing intently on the section of floor in front of him. "You've got good instincts for this," he said after a moment. "Most people would be pushing too hard, trying to force it."

"Oh? What's the right way?" Ava asked, genuinely curious. In Chicago, she'd overseen plenty of renovations, but she'd never actually *done* the work herself. That was what contractors were for.

Liam sat back, wiping his forehead with the back of his arm. The gesture pulled his t-shirt tight across his shoulders, and Ava forced herself to look at the floor instead.

"With the grain," he said, running his palm across a section he'd just finished. The gesture was almost tender. "See how it runs? You have to read it first, understand what direction the wood wants to go. If you fight it, you'll just tear it up. But if you work with it..." He pressed his sanding block down and moved it smoothly along the grain line. The wood seemed to *respond*, brightening under his touch. "The wood tells you what it wants to be."

Ava watched his hands—strong and skilful, moving with surprising gentleness. The hands of a master craftsman. "What does this wood want to be?"

"Beautiful." He said it without hesitation, without irony. "It wants to be exactly what it was meant to be from the beginning. We just have to help it remember."

Something in Ava's chest twisted painfully. When was the last time anyone had talked about *her* like that? Like she had an essential nature that just needed to be uncovered, rather than a series of flaws that needed to be fixed? She bent back to her work, but the words kept echoing in her mind. *Work with the grain, not against it.* How much of her life had she spent fighting against her own grain, trying to force herself into shapes that didn't fit?

"I'm glad I decided to restore this house, and keep what we could. It's taken longer in some cases, and the lack of granite counter top is hurting the resale, but I'm really glad we...I decided to bring it back to life not replace it. Even if it takes longer, and costs more."

"And might reduce your profits when you sell," he added.

"*If* I sell." She corrected, before she even realized she was speaking.

If? Really? she thought.

For a long moment, Liam didn't move. Then, slowly, a smile spread across his face, not the sardonic smirk she'd gotten used to, but something genuine and a little bit awed. "I'm glad too." he said softly.

They stared at each other. The work stopped. The hallway seemed to have shrunk as it was even smaller than before. The space between them was charged with possibility. There was sawdust caught in Liam's eyelashes, pale wood a contrast to the different shades of green and gold in his eyes in the harsh light of the work lamps.

"Ava" Liam started, his voice rough.

He moved closer, or maybe she did. All she knew was that suddenly he was *there*, so close she could feel the heat radiating off his skin, could smell sawdust and sweat and something essentially *him*. Finally this is it, she thought.

His hand came up slowly, giving her every chance to pull away. When she didn't, his fingers brushed her forehead, feather-light.

"You've got dust," he murmured, his thumb wiping gently at her skin. But he didn't pull away. His hand lingered, cupping the side of her face, and Ava found herself leaning into the touch like a flower turning toward the sun.

His eyes darkened. He leaned in, and Ava's eyes started to flutter closed, her whole body tensing in anticipation—

BZZZZZZT. BZZZZZZT. BZZZZZZT.

The violent vibration of her phone against the wooden crate where she'd left it shattered the moment like a rock through glass.

BZZZZZZT. BZZZZZZT. BZZZZZZT.

Ava jerked back instinctively, her hand flying to her chest as if to calm her racing heart.

BZZZZZZT. BZZZZZZT. BZZZZZZT.

The phone continued its angry dance, buzzing and lighting up the dim hallway with cold blue light. Ava saw the caller ID on the screen.

Martin - Mobile

Her blood turned to ice.

BZZZZZZT. BZZZZZZT. BZZZZZZT.

Liam saw it too. A second passed. A second where she could have turned the phone over, or said "ignore it" but the second passed too quickly and in her hesitation, the moment took a different course.

"You should get that," Liam said, his voice flat. He was already pulling back, the warmth draining from his expression like water from a broken cup.

"I..." Ava started, but the protest died on her lips, like the moment that had just withered between them. Because the truth was, her body had already betrayed her. The moment she'd seen Martin's name, every muscle in her body had tensed with a Pavlovian response cultivated over six years of being at his beck and call, and Liam had obviously sensed it. The *Martin Reflex*, Maya had called it. The inability to let a work call go unanswered, no matter the hour, no matter the situation.

Her hand was already reaching for the phone on autopilot.

Liam saw it. She watched his face shutter completely before she could pull her hand away, that grumpy mask she'd grown to hate slamming back into place.

"Liam..." she started. But she knew she'd missed her opportunity to save this.

"I said you should take it." He was already standing, his voice was calm but he was wiping his dusty hands on his jeans with jerky, angry movements. "Sounds important." And he left the hall.

The phone kept buzzing, insistent, demanding. Ava stared at it like it was a snake coiled on the crate. Eventually it stopped.

"I'm done for the night anyway," Liam said, coming back into the room, his voice like pleasant, but cold as ice. He started gathering his tools with sharp, efficient movements, not looking at her. "Early start tomorrow. Sophie needs help with something at the bookstore."

"Liam." Ava stood too, dust falling from her jeans in small clouds. "Please, just..."

"What?" He finally looked at her, and the distance in his eyes made her chest ache. "Just wait while you take a call from your real life?"

She wasn't expecting the sharpness in his reply. "That's not fair."

He put his hand up, a gesture that said he didn't want to argue, and as he did the phone started buzzing again. "Your boss calls at midnight and you can't *not* answer? That tells me everything I need to know."

"It wasn't...You don't..."

"I understand." Liam's voice was bitter. "I've been here before, remember? I'm the guy people leave behind. The local fix-it man who's good enough for a project, or a fling while you're slumming it in a small town, but not good enough to choose when your real life comes calling."

The words hit Ava like a slap. "Is that really what you think? That this is some kind of a...a vacation romance for me?"

"Isn't it?" Liam challenged. "You've been here, what, three weeks? You're talking about restoration like you're going to stay, like you're going to see it through. Saying 'if' not 'when' you'll sell. But we both know how this ends, Ava. You're going to finish the house, or hell, maybe you won't even finish it. Maybe you'll get a better offer and sell it as-is. Either way, you're going back to Chicago. To your glass towers and your important deals and your midnight phone calls."

The phone started buzzing again. Third time.

"Answer it," Liam said quietly, and the resignation in his voice was somehow worse than the anger. "I'll see you tomorrow. If you're still here."

He walked out and headed for the front door. Ava stood frozen in the hallway, surrounded by the evidence of their evening's work, the beautiful wood they'd uncovered together, the dust coating every surface, the work lamps casting harsh shadows that suddenly seemed cruel rather than practical.

The door closed behind Liam with a soft click more final than a slam.

Ava's phone went silent, then immediately started buzzing again.

With shaking hands, she picked it up and swiped to answer.

"Martin." Her voice came out flat, empty.

"Ava! Thank God. I've been trying to reach you for hours." Martin's voice filled her ear, as familiar and unwelcome as an old injury. "Listen, I know it's late, but I need to talk to you. Are you somewhere you can speak freely?"

Ava looked around at the space where Liam had been kneeling just moments ago. She could still feel the ghost of his touch on her forehead.

"I'm alone," she said.

"Good. Good." Martin let out a breath. "Ava, I think we made a big mistake."

The words hung in the air between Chicago and Willow Creek, heavy with implication.

"What kind of mistake?" Ava asked, though part of her didn't want to know.

"The West Side deal. Letting you go for a month. All of it." Martin's words came faster now, tumbling over themselves. "I've had time to think, and I was wrong. The firm was wrong. You're too valuable to lose, especially for a project as big as the West Side development."

Ava sat down hard on a nearby crate, dust puffing up around her.

"What are you saying, Martin?"

"I'm saying we want you to come back. I want you to come back. Now. I've talked to the partners, and we're prepared to make you a very generous offer. Bring you up to partner Ava. Your own team. First crack at the Lincoln Park portfolio that's coming up. It's huge, easily twice the size of the West Side deal."

The words should have filled her with elation. Three weeks ago they would have. Partner. Her own team. The Lincoln Park portfolio. Moving up.

But not out, she thought. Do you really want to go back?

All she could think about was the way Liam's hand had softly caressed her face. The way he'd looked at her when she'd said she wanted the house to breathe.

"I need time," she heard herself say.

"Of course, of course," Martin said quickly. "But not too much time. We need an answer soonish. The partners are eager to move forward, and if you're not interested, we'll need to start looking at other candidates..."

"I said I need time, Martin." Ava's voice came out sharper than she'd intended. "I'll call you Monday."

She hung up before he could respond, cutting off his protests mid-sentence.

The hallway was silent again, but it felt different now. The magic that had filled it just minutes ago was gone, replaced by a cold, harsh reality. Ava looked down at the phone in her hand, the same phone that had been buzzing all week with updates from her realtor, with emails from her mother asking when she was coming home, with reminders of the life she'd left behind.

The life that was apparently waiting for her to come back.

Partner. Her own team.

And all she had to do was leave Willow Creek. Leave the house. Leave the beautiful oak floors that were just beginning to reveal themselves. Leave Mama C and her coffee. Leave the quiet mornings watching sunrise over the orchard.

Leave Liam.

Ava set the phone down on the crate like it might burn her and looked around the hallway with new eyes. In the harsh light of the work lamps, every imperfection stood out. The sections they hadn't sanded yet, the water stains that might never fully come out, the boards that would need to be replaced entirely. It was a mess. A beautiful, impossible mess.

Just like her life.

She thought about what Liam had said about working with the grain. About not forcing things, but letting them become what they were meant to be.

What was she meant to be?

She ran her hand over the section of floor she'd been working on, feeling the smooth wood under her palm. She'd done this. She'd uncovered this beauty with her own hands, her own labor. Not by delegating to a contractor or writing a check, but by getting down on her knees and doing the work. When was the last time she'd created something beautiful with her own hands in Chicago? When was the last time she'd been this *alive*?

But Liam's words echoed in her mind too: *I'm the guy people leave behind.*

And the worst part was, she couldn't promise him he was wrong. Could she really give up everything she'd worked for? Could she really choose a half-finished house in a town of 2,000 people over a senior position at one of Chicago's top architecture firms?

Could she choose Liam over her career?

Ava sat in the hallway until the work lamps started to hurt her eyes, until the dust settled on every surface, until her phone buzzed again, this time with a text from Martin: *Think about it, Ava. This is your second chance. Don't waste it.*

She turned off the lamps one by one, plunging the hallway into darkness. But even in the dark, she could feel the beautiful wood beneath her feet, solid and true, waiting patiently for her to decide who she wanted to be.

The Foundation of Doubt

The cottage was cold.

Ava woke to the kind of penetrating chill that made her bones ache, the kind that no amount of blankets could chase away. She'd turned the heat down before bed, some misguided attempt at punishing herself for the disaster that had been last night's phone call. Or maybe she'd wanted to punish the house itself, this beautiful trap that was making her forget who she was supposed to be.

She pulled on yesterday's jeans and the flannel Liam had lent her weeks ago, the one she kept meaning to give back but somehow never did. The fabric still smelled faintly of sawdust and...something warm that made her chest hurt.

Stop it, she told herself. *You're being ridiculous.*

But she couldn't stop thinking about the look on Liam's face when he'd left. The way his jaw had tightened, his eyes going carefully blank. She'd seen that expression before, the professional mask people wore when they were too proud to show they'd been hurt. She'd never expected to see it on Liam. He was cold and grumpy, but she had managed to remove that. And last night, she forced him to put it back on.

By the time she made it downstairs, her coffee maker sputtering to life in the kitchen, she heard his truck pull up. The engine cut off with a decisive finality that made her stomach clench. Through the window, she watched him gather his tools with mechanical efficiency. No pause. No glance toward the house. Just clipboards and measuring tape and the kind of focused determination that looked a lot like anger wrapped in professionalism.

She poured her coffee, black, because she'd forgotten to buy cream and because, well, that was how Liam liked it and she was beginning to like it too. And she waited.

When Liam knocked, it was perfunctory. Three sharp raps, no rhythm to them.

"Morning," he said curtly when he opened the door. His eyes didn't quite meet hers, landing somewhere over her left shoulder. "We need to get started on the staircase today. It's the last big job and it'll take a while."

No thermos in his hand. No easy smile. Just business.

"Right," Ava said, hating how small her voice sounded. "The staircase."

He was already moving past her, bootprints tracking across the floor she'd swept last night in a futile attempt to distract herself from replaying every word of Martin's call. Liam headed straight for the central hallway, where the grand staircase curved upward like a spine, the literal backbone of the house.

Ava followed, coffee cup clutched between her hands like a lifeline.

The staircase was in worse shape than she'd realized. Several of the balusters were missing entirely, and the handrail had separated from the newel post at the bottom, leaving the whole structure unstable. Liam had already laid out his tools with mathematical precision: levels, squares, clamps, a miter saw set up in the corner with an extension cord snaking back to the kitchen.

"We'll need to remove the existing handrail system completely," he said, his voice flat and instructional. "The structural posts are sound, but the connections are shot. We'll have to match the existing profile for the new balusters. I've got the router bits we'll need, but it's going to be tedious work."

His voice was cold and clipped. Ava missed the Liam she had gotten to know, now she was back at Liam on the first day. She nodded, setting her coffee aside. "Tell me what you need me to do."

For the next hour, they worked in near silence. Not the comfortable silence of sanding the hallway floor, the awkward silence of two people purposefully not speaking to each other. Liam showed her how to carefully remove the old balusters without damaging the mortises in the handrail, his hands demonstrating the technique with clinical efficiency. No casual touches though. No shared laughter when she nearly dropped a baluster. Just the sound of wood against wood and the occasional terse instruction.

"Hold this steady while I drill out the dowel."

"Hand me the chisel. The half-inch, not the quarter."

"You need to support the rail from underneath or it'll crack."

It was professional. Practical. Completely devoid of the warmth that had grown between them.

Ava's chest tightened with words she didn't know how to say. *I'm sorry* seemed inadequate. *It wasn't what you think* was probably a lie. *Please look at me* was too desperate. So she said nothing, and the silence stretched between them like a fault line.

By mid-morning, they'd moved on to the most crucial part of the work: realigning the main handrail to the newel posts. It was precision work that required both of them, one person to hold the heavy oak rail at exactly the right angle while the other secured it. The kind of task that demanded trust, communication, perfect synchronization.

They had none of those things today.

"Lift your end another quarter inch," Liam said in his gruff voice, checking his level for the third time.

Ava adjusted her grip, her arms already shaking from holding the awkward angle. The rail had to weigh sixty pounds, all of it concentrated in a six-foot section of solid wood.

"That's too much. Down a fraction."

She lowered it slightly, sweat starting to bead on her forehead despite the cold.

"No, now it's..." He stopped himself, his lips flattened into a thin line. "Just... hold it steady for a second."

But Ava's arms were trembling, and the rail shifted. Just a fraction, just enough to throw off his measurement.

"Ava." His voice was tight. "I need you to keep it still."

"I'm trying," she snapped back, frustration and exhaustion and guilt all bubbling up at once. "It's heavy, and you keep changing your mind about where you want it."

"I'm not changing my mind. I'm trying to get it level. It's kind of important for a staircase."

"Well, maybe if you actually communicated what you needed instead of just barking adjustments..."

"I am communicating. You're just not listening."

The rail slipped in her hands. Liam lunged forward to catch it, and for a terrible moment, they were both struggling with the weight, the heavy oak swinging between them like a pendulum. If it fell wrong, if it hit one of them, if the newel post cracked under the stress...

"Down!" Liam commanded, and they lowered it together to the floor, breathing hard.

The silence that followed was worse than the argument.

Liam straightened, breathing hard and running a hand through his hair. "This isn't safe."

"I know." Ava's arms were still shaking. "I'm sorry, I just..."

"We need to be in sync for this kind of work." He was looking at the staircase, not at her. "If we can't communicate, someone's going to get hurt."

The words hung between them, meaning more than just the physical task at hand.

Ava opened her mouth, closed it. What could she say? That she'd spent the entire morning wanting to explain about Martin, about Chicago, about the life she'd left behind that kept reaching out to pull her back? How torn she was? That she was terrified by how much last night had hurt, not the phone call, but seeing Liam's face when he heard her slipping back into Executive Ava, all clipped efficiency and professional distance?

That she didn't know how to be both versions of herself at once?

"I need some air," she said instead. "Run into town for a bit. Clear my head."

Liam nodded, already turning back to his tools. "Good idea."

She waited, just for a second, hoping he'd ask her to stay. Hoping he'd look at her the way he had last night before everything went wrong, like she was something precious and real and worth fighting for. But he just picked up his tape measure and started taking notes on his clipboard, his handwriting precise and controlled.

Ava grabbed her jacket and left.

The drive into town should have cleared her head. Instead, it gave her too much time to think.

Her phone sat in the passenger seat, silent. She'd turned off notifications after the fifth text from Martin had buzzed through this morning. She didn't need to read them to know what they said: '*Where are you?*' and '*We need to talk about the timeline*' and '*You can't just ignore me, Ava.*'

The thing was, she could. She'd been ignoring things for years, her mother's concerns about her work-life balance, her friends' suggestions that she was burning out, the small voice in her head that whispered she was building someone else's dream instead of her own. Ignoring things was easy. Facing them was hard.

Willow Creek's town square was quiet on a Tuesday morning, just a handful of cars parked along Main Street. Ava found a spot in front of the general store and sat for a moment, watching people move through their daily routines. Mrs Avery from the post office chatting with someone outside Sophie's bookstore. A couple of teenagers skateboarding past the war memorial. Normal life, the kind that didn't involve seven-figure budgets or impossible deadlines or choosing between the person you used to be and the person you might become.

She was reaching for the door handle when someone rapped on her window.

Silas grinned at her through the glass, his weathered face creasing with amusement. "You planning to sit in that car all day, or are you coming in for coffee?"

Ava couldn't help but smile as she climbed out. "Is it that obvious I need coffee?"

"Honey, you look like you need a whole lot more than coffee, but it's a start." He gestured toward Mama C's diner. "Come on. Mama C's making her Tuesday special, and she'll have my hide if I don't deliver you to her."

The diner was warm and smelled like bacon and fresh bread. And coffee. Wonderful coffee. Mama C took one look at Ava's face and pointed to a booth in the corner, the kind with high backs that created a little bubble of privacy.

"Sit," she commanded. "I'll bring you the good coffee."

When she returned, she slid into the booth across from Ava, her dark eyes knowing. Silas joined them, setting down a plate of what looked like homemade cinnamon rolls.

"So," Mama C said. "You want to tell us what's got you looking like someone kicked your puppy, or should I just start guessing?"

Ava wrapped her hands around the coffee mug. "Is it that obvious?"

"Sweetheart, you've got 'relationship trouble' written all over your face." Mama C exchanged a glance with Silas. "And since the only person you've been spending time with is our Liam, I'm guessing this has something to do with him."

"We're not..." Ava stopped. Were they in a relationship? They'd shared moments. They'd almost kissed. But they'd never actually talked about what was happening between them. "It's complicated."

"It always is," Silas said, his voice gentle. "But complicated doesn't mean impossible."

Mama C leaned forward. "Did he do something stupid? Because if he did, I'll straighten him out. I changed that boy's diapers, he'll listen to me."

Despite everything, Ava laughed. "No, he didn't, it's not his fault. It's mine. I got a phone call last night, from my old life in Chicago, and I just...I went right back into work mode. And Liam, he just shut down."

"Mmmmmm." Mama C nodded slowly. "The past came calling."

"Something like that."

For a long moment, no one spoke. Then Mama C reached across the table and covered Ava's hand with her own. "Let me tell you something about this cottage you're fixing up," she said. "About Beatrice, the woman who built it. Married, but never had any children, and her husband died young. Word is, it was never a particularly happy marriage. As is often the way, it was a good marriage, from the family's point of view but..."

"Rumor has it she had a lover," Silas cut in, quietly. "Someone she couldn't acknowledge publicly. Different times back then, more judgment."

Mama C nodded. "Her husband was a respectable man, good family, left her some money. She bought that land on the ridge and the old original cottage on it. Then with her own two hands, turned that little thing into the quaint little country house you see today. Well, her hands and a whole lot of help from a certain carpenter in town. They worked on that house for years. Built it and rebuilt it room by room, every detail perfect at her direction. She was a force of nature, but she was doing it alone."

Knowing the truth between Thomas and Aunt Bea, Ava smiled.

Mama C continued. "Never remarried. Lived most of her life alone. I don't think she ever told her beau what he meant to her, never made a choice between her old 'respectable' life, and the new one she was building. Where she could live on her own terms. And be happy."

"And what happened?" Ava asked innocently.

"He would have waited," Silas said. "Longer than most men would have I'm sure. But you can't build a foundation on uncertainty, and he got tired of wondering if she'd ever actually choose him."

"She made the choice to live as society expected, as her family had wanted, and she would have lost what could have been the love of her life because she wasn't willing to make a decision and choose happiness. She got a great house. But a quiet one." Mama C finished.

The words settled over Ava like a weight. Knowing what she did about Thomas and Aunt Bea's 'enduring friendship' she knew they did have the love affair Mama C was speaking of, albeit a love affair through words and imagination. Working on the house and making it their dream home, but still, never actually able to share that space together as they wanted. Two lovers kept apart by society and respectability. It may not have been as empty a life as Mama C made out, but it wasn't...complete.

She looked down at her coffee, seeing her reflection distorted in the dark surface.

"Silence is the only thing that rots a house faster than water," Mama C said softly. "Remember that."

Ava thought about her situation with Liam. Was she like Aunt Bea? Trapped between two worlds, Chicago and Willow Creek? Was this her one and potentially only opportunity to make a call to pick one and go down a path of happiness? If she didn't, would she and Liam end up writing dozens of letters to each making up a life they never got to have, all because she never had the guts to make a call and tell Chicago, tell Martin, tell the bank and the finance companies no? That she chose love. And small town gossip. And Mama C's coffee.

After they'd finished their coffee and Ava had picked at a cinnamon roll she couldn't taste, she excused herself to use the restroom. On the way back, she caught sight of herself in the diner's front window. For a moment, she didn't recognize the woman looking back at her.

She was wearing Liam's yellow flannel, with the frayed cuffs that she'd claimed as her own somewhere along the way. Her hair was in a messy knot, loose strands falling around her face. Her hands, reflected in the glass, were marked with small cuts and calluses from the renovation work. She looked tired, yes, but there was something else too. A softness around her eyes that hadn't been there in Chicago. A hint of color in her cheeks from all the time spent working outdoors.

She looked... happy. Or at least, she had until she'd let Chicago back in.

Executive Ava, the woman in pressed suits who commanded board-rooms and juggled impossible deadlines, was nowhere to be seen. That woman was a stranger now, someone she'd been pretending to be for so long that she'd forgotten it was a performance. This woman, the one in work clothes with sawdust probably still in her hair, was more real, more solid than Executive Ava had ever been. Which one was she willing to fight for?

By the time Ava pulled back up to the cottage, the sun was already starting to sink toward the horizon, painting the sky her favorite shades of amber and rose. She'd driven around for hours after leaving the diner, following country roads she'd never explored, trying to sort through the tangle of emotions in her chest.

Liam's truck was still there.

She found him in the hallway, still working on the staircase. He'd made significant progress. Several new balusters were in place, their fresh-cut wood pale against the aged oak of the existing structure. He was on his knees, fitting another piece, his movements precise and con-trolled, like a maestro conducting an orchestra of woodworking tools.

He didn't look up when she came in.

"You're still here," she said.

"Wanted to get the structural supports in place before I left." His voice was neutral, professional. "It's not safe to leave the rail unsecured overnight."

Ava watched him work for a moment, this man who cared so much about doing things right. Who'd spent his evening making sure her house was safe, even though she'd hurt him. Even though he had every right to pack up his tools and leave.

Her heart was suddenly too big for her chest.

"I blocked Martin's number," she said.

Liam's hands stilled. He didn't look up, but she saw his shoulders tense.

"Why?"

"I want to." The words came out stronger than she'd expected. "He's...telling me how much the firm needs me, how I'm wasting my potential out here." She took a breath. "And I took his call because some part of me is terrified that if I don't, I'll just be... this. Someone fixing up an old cottage in a town nobody's heard of."

Finally, Liam looked at her. His eyes were guarded, but there was something else there too, a flicker of hope he was trying hard to hide. "And what's wrong with that?" he asked quietly, focussing on the bannister.

"Nothing." Ava said with a hint of panic. "That's what scares me. There's nothing wrong with it, and I don't know how to be the kind of person who's okay with that."

The silence stretched between them, but it was different now. Not angry, not cold. Expectant, like the moment before a storm breaks.

Liam stood slowly, brushing sawdust from his jeans. "The staircase," he said, gesturing to the half-finished rail. "I can't do the next part alone. Need someone to hold the level while I secure the connection points."

It wasn't an answer to her confession. It wasn't forgiveness or a declaration. But it was an invitation, a tentative bridge back to the partnership they'd built.

Ava stepped forward. "Show me what you need."

They worked in the fading light, their movements careful and deliberate. Liam positioned the level against the handrail, and Ava held the other end, keeping it steady while he checked the bubble. This time, when he adjusted the angle, he told her exactly what he needed. This time, when her arms started to shake, she told him she needed a break.

Communication. Trust. The foundations they'd been building all along.

"There," Liam said finally, securing the last bracket. "That should hold."

He stepped back to examine their work, and Ava did the same. The staircase wasn't finished, there were still balusters to install, details to re-fine, but the structure was sound. The backbone was strong.

"It's good work," she said.

"Yeah." Liam glanced at her, and for the first time all day, the smallest flicker of that almost smile he had. "We make a good team."

"When we're not being stubborn idiots."

"Especially then."

The almost-smile became a real one, and Ava relaxed. They weren't fixed, there were still conversations to be had, decisions to be made. But they were here, standing in the house they were rebuilding together, and that had to count for something.

Liam started gathering his tools, moving with the easy efficiency of someone who'd done this a thousand times. "I should head out. It's getting dark."

"Liam." Ava waited until he looked at her. "Thank you. For staying. For... not giving up on this. I'm sorry I... I got scared."

He studied her for a long moment, his expression unreadable. Then he shouldered his tool bag and headed for the door. At the threshold, he paused. "I'm not the one you need to worry about giving up, Ava," he said quietly. "I know what I want."

The implication hung in the air: *Do you?*

Then he was gone, his truck rumbling to life in the driveway, tail-lights disappearing down the ridge road.

Ava stood in the doorway of her cottage, *her* cottage, not Beatrice's, not Chicago's, hers, and watched until the lights faded completely. The evening air was cold against her face, sharp and clean. Inside, the house waited. The staircase they'd built together, strong and true. The floors they'd sanded, the walls they'd patched. Every room was a choice she'd made to stay, to try, to become someone new.

She went inside and closed the door on the cold.

Willow Creek Waltz

Ava stood in the middle of the cottage bedroom, hands on her hips, staring at the meager contents of her open suitcase with growing frustration. She'd packed light when she'd left Chicago almost four weeks ago. Just enough time to flip the property and get back to her real life.

She hadn't packed for a town dance.

Apparently a fall tradition, it was the kind of thing that made Ava squirm. Not just because the concept of an entire town getting together for a festival seemed just too quaint to be real, the thought of crowds of people, most of them strangers, but all of them looking at her like she was the biggest stranger there, sent a wave of panic through her system. Still, when Mama C had mentioned it at the diner Liam was particularly enthusiastic that Ava should attend, and while cloaked in a 'going away' party vibe, she hoped it was said with the hope of more of an opportunity to spend personal time together outside of the cottage.

Spread across the freshly refinished dresser were her options: a sleek black sheath dress with an architectural neckline that screamed *corporate event*, a pair of dark jeans that were more *business casual Friday* than *romantic evening*, and a cream silk blouse that would look ridiculous paired with anything she owned. Every piece was tailored, structured, designed to project power and competence in glass-walled conference rooms.

Nothing said *dance under the stars in a small town.*

"This is ridiculous," she pouted, holding up the black dress. It was beautiful in its way, expensive, minimalist, the kind of thing she'd wear to a gallery opening or client dinner. Here, in this cottage with its exposed beams and rustic charm, it looked like a costume from another planet. She glanced at the clock on her phone. Four hours until the dance. Four hours to find something that wouldn't make her stick out like a sore thumb in a community that had *finally* started to accept her as more than just "the city girl."

With a frustrated sigh, she grabbed her keys and headed into town.

The Willow Creek town square was already transforming when Ava arrived.

She parked her car near Mama's Diner and stepped out into the golden afternoon light, immediately drawn to the activity buzzing around the central plaza. The scent of fresh-cut pine and honeysuckle drifted on the warm breeze, mixing with something else, barbecue smoke from the pit being set up near the gazebo. Strings of white lights were being draped between the ancient oak trees by a group of men on ladders, their easy laughter carrying across the square. Mrs Gable directed traffic from below, pointing and calling out instructions with the authority of a battlefield general. Children ran between the workers, their excitement palpable as they watched their small town dress up for the evening.

Ava found herself smiling and drawn to it like a moth to a flame, taking it all in.

Long tables were being set up along one side, covered in checkered cloths that fluttered in the breeze. She recognized Silas organising the arrangement of hay bales for additional seating, while a younger couple assembled what looked like a small stage near the gazebo. Instruments were being unloaded from a truck, a fiddle case, a guitar, what might have been a banjo.

A banjo! You don't get those in Chicago, and Ava surprised herself that she had seen a banjo and not been immediately repulsed.

It was charming in a way that had nothing to do with careful event planning or hired coordinators. This was a community coming together, everyone contributing, everyone invested in creating something beautiful for their neighbors. So different from the sterile corporate events she was used to, catered affairs in hotel ballrooms, everything outsourced and impersonal, attended by people who were there to network rather than connect.

"Looking good, isn't it?"

Ava turned to find Silas approaching, wiping his hands on his jeans. His weathered face creased into a warm smile. She caught him off guard slightly. The man moved like a cat. "It's beautiful," she said honestly. "You all do this every year?"

"Every spring and every fall. Been a tradition since before I was born." He gestured toward the gazebo, where the fairy lights were beginning to create a canopy of stars even in the afternoon sun. "My Vera and I had our first dance right there, sixty-two years ago." His eyes went distant with memory, soft with affection. "These dances, they're where life happens in Willow Creek. First kisses, proposals... reconciliations," he said with a meaningful look, "all under those lights."

Something tightened in Ava's chest. "That's really special."

"You coming tonight of course." It wasn't a question, as Silas' knowing smile suggested he already knew the answer.

"I'm planning to. If I can find something appropriate to wear." She gestured ruefully at her current outfit, work jeans and Liam's flannel shirt, both covered in a fine layer of sawdust from the never ending sanding of the cottage floors.

Silas chuckled. "Well, I reckon Mama C might be able to help you with that. She's got a knack for solving problems." He tipped his hat. "You should stop by the diner. I believe she's expecting the usual afternoon rush about now."

It wasn't subtle, but Ava found she didn't mind. She thanked him and made her way toward the diner, her boots clicking against the sidewalk as she passed storefronts she was beginning to recognize. The Dust

Jacket with its window display of local authors, the small gallery that featured works by regional artists. Three weeks ago, this had all been foreign territory. Now, it was starting to feel like home.

The thought should have terrified her. Instead, it settled warm and right in her chest.

The bell above Mama's Diner chimed as Ava pushed through the door, and she was immediately enveloped by the familiar scents of coffee, fresh-baked bread, and bacon, that made her stomach rumble despite the sandwich she'd eaten for lunch.

The afternoon crowd was lighter than the breakfast rush she'd witnessed a few times, a couple of local farmers at the counter, a young family in one of the booths, two elderly women sharing a pot of tea by the window. All eyes turned to her as she entered, but the looks were friendly now, accompanied by nods and small waves. She'd earned that, she realized. Weeks of hard work, of proving she wasn't just playing at renovation, of showing up day after day covered in dust and determination. Willow Creek was a town that valued effort, and she'd finally passed whatever invisible test they'd been administering.

"Well, look what the cat dragged in!" Mama C's voice boomed from behind the counter, warm and welcoming. "Sugar, you look like you could use some coffee and a slice of pie."

"Just coffee would be great," Ava said, sliding onto one of the chrome-topped stools. "Though I've never said no to your pie."

"Cherry today. Fresh this morning." Mama C was already pouring coffee into a thick ceramic mug. "You taking a break from the cottage? Liam told me you two have been working like dogs to get the floors done."

"Finished about an hour ago." Ava wrapped her hands around the warm mug, letting the heat seep into her perpetually sore muscles. "They look incredible. The original hardwood came up beautiful once we got through all the layers of old carpet and linoleum."

"That's wonderful, honey." Mama C set a generous slice of pie in front of her, steam still rising from the latticed crust. "So you'll be at the dance tonight then? Celebrating?"

Ava sighed, poking at the pie with her fork. "That's the plan. If I can find something to wear that doesn't make me look like I'm heading to a board meeting or a construction site."

Mama C's eyes sparkled with interest. "Having wardrobe troubles?"

"That's putting it mildly." Ava took a bite of pie and nearly moaned. God, the woman was a wizard in the kitchen. "I packed for a 30 day renovation project, not a social calendar. And even if some of it was the right choice for a renovation" she said, thinking of those boots she wore on the first day, "everything I brought is either covered in paint or completely inappropriate for a town dance."

"Hmm." Mama C leaned against the counter, studying Ava with an assessing eye that made her feel like she was being measured for something. "What size are you, sugar? About a six?"

"Usually. Why?"

A slow smile spread across Mama C's face, the kind that suggested she was about to solve a problem Ava hadn't fully articulated. "Finish that pie and come with me. I think I might have something that'll work perfectly."

"Mama C, I couldn't—"

"Hush now. You can and you will." The older woman untied her apron and called toward the kitchen. "Jenny! Watch the counter for a few minutes?"

A young waitress appeared, nodding enthusiastically. "Of course, Mama C!"

Before Ava could protest further, she found herself being ushered out of the diner and up the narrow staircase that led to the apartment above. She'd never been up here before, this was Mama C's private space, separate from the public face of the diner.

The apartment was exactly what Ava would have expected: cozy and warm, filled with photographs and comfortable furniture that had clearly been chosen for living rather than style. Crocheted afghans draped over the sofa, plants thrived on every available windowsill, and the walls were covered with framed pictures of Mama C's children at various ages, Mama C with a man who must have been her late husband, what looked like three generations of family gatherings.

"This way, sugar." Mama C led her down a short hallway to a guest room done in soft florals and cream. She moved to the closet with purpose, pulling out a garment bag that she handled with obvious reverence.

"This was my daughter-in-law's," she said softly, laying the bag across the bed. "Diana. She wore it to the Harvest Dance the year she and Robert fell in love." Her voice caught slightly before steadying. "That girl had taste, I'll give her that. And she was about your size."

Ava's throat tightened. "Mama C, I can't wear—"

"Yes, you can!" The older woman's tone was gentle but firm. "It's been hanging in this closet for five years, and your Aunt Beatrice would roll over in her grave if she knew I was letting perfectly good clothing go to waste." She turned to face Ava, her eyes warm and knowing. "Besides, I've seen the way Liam looks at you when you're covered in sawdust and swearing at stuck windows. I can only imagine what'll happen when you clean up proper."

Heat flooded Ava's cheeks. "We're just..."

"'Working together' I know. But sugar, I've been watching people fall in love in this town for sixty years." Mama C patted her hand. "I know what I'm seeing. And I know our Liam. That boy hasn't looked at anyone the way he looks at you since... well. Since Beatrice passed, he hasn't looked at anyone much at all." She squeezed Ava's fingers. "You're good for him. You make him remember there's more to life than grief and obligation."

The words hit Ava square in the chest, stealing her breath. She wanted to argue, but none of those protests made it past her lips. Because the truth was, she was already falling. Had been falling since the moment he'd handed her a sledgehammer and challenged her to prove she belonged. She was almost embarrassed it had taken her this long to acknowledge it and what she needed to do to make it real.

"Now," Mama C said, unzipping the garment bag with a flourish, "let's see if this fits."

The dress was beautiful.

Soft sage green fabric the color of new spring leaves spilled from the bag, flowing like water as Mama C lifted it out. The bodice was fitted but not restrictive, with delicate cap sleeves that would leave shoulders bare. The skirt fell in gentle layers that would move when she walked, feminine and free in a way Ava's structured pieces never allowed. It was the opposite of everything in her Chicago wardrobe.

It was perfect.

"Go on," Mama C urged, draping the dress over Ava's arms. "Try it on. Bathroom's right through there."

Five minutes later, Ava stood in front of the full-length mirror in Mama C's guest room and barely recognized herself.

The woman staring back wasn't Executive Ava Gardiner, terror of the boardroom, master of the fifteen-minute power pitch. This woman had sun-kissed shoulders that showed the subtle definition of new muscle earned through weeks of honest labor. Her arms, once pale and thin from too many hours under fluorescent lights, now carried a golden tan and the strength that came from swinging hammers and hauling lumber. The dress hugged curves she'd forgotten she had, curves that power suits had been designed to minimize, to make her less soft, less feminine, less *available* to be dismissed as anything other than formidable.

But it was her face that startled her most. Her cheeks held color that had nothing to do with expensive blush. Her eyes were bright, alive in a way they hadn't been in years. She looked like a woman who laughed over paint samples and danced in sawdust and wasn't afraid to get her hands dirty. She looked like a woman who might belong in Willow Creek. The realization settled in her chest with an ache that was equal parts terrifying and thrilling.

"Oh, sugar." Mama C appeared in the doorway, one hand pressed to her heart. "You look just beautiful. Beatrice would've loved to see this."

"I don't know how to be this person," Ava whispered, still staring at her reflection.

"You already are this person. You have been for weeks now." Mama C came to stand behind her, meeting her eyes in the mirror. "The only difference is now you're letting her show on the outside too."

Ava touched the soft fabric at her waist, watched the way it moved with her. "I'm not dressing for a board meeting."

"Oh no, honey. You're not." Mama C's smile was knowing, kind. "You're dressing for a man who has seen you at your absolute worst, covered in grime, frustrated with plumbing, cursing a blue streak, and still looks at you like you hung the moon."

The truth of it made Ava's eyes sting. She blinked rapidly, trying to maintain composure.

"Now." Mama C squeezed her shoulders. "You've got a few hours before the dance starts. Go home, take a long bath in that gorgeous clawfoot tub you and Liam just installed, do whatever it is you city girls do to feel pretty. And then tonight..." Her eyes twinkled. "Tonight, you show Willow Creek exactly who Ava Gardiner really is."

The Willow Creek town square at dusk was even more magical than it had been that afternoon.

The fairy lights that had looked charming in daylight now glowed like captured stars against the darkening sky, creating a canopy of warm light that transformed the entire plaza into something out of a storybook. The scent of slow-smoked barbecue was stronger now, making Ava's mouth water as she approached. The long tables were laden with covered dishes, the town's potluck tradition in full force, and the sound of the folk band tuning their instruments drifted across the square, mixing with laughter and conversation.

Children still ran between the adults, though their earlier wild energy had been channeled into something slightly more controlled. Families had claimed spots on quilts spread across the grass, or at gathered hay bales. Neighbors greeted neighbors with the easy familiarity of people who'd known each other for decades.

Ava paused at the edge of the square, suddenly uncertain.

In Chicago, she knew how to make an entrance, chin up, shoulders back, own the room before it owned you. But here, in this borrowed dress that had belonged to a woman she'd never met, about to step into a community that had watched her struggle and sweat and probably laughed at her incompetence more than once, she was vulnerable in a way no boardroom had ever managed.

Then she saw him.

Liam stood near the barbecue pit, shoulders tense in a way that suggested he was about as comfortable with this social gathering as she was. He'd traded his usual flannel and work jeans for dark denim and a button-down shirt in deep blue that strained slightly across his broad shoulders. He'd made an attempt to tame his perpetually messy hair, though one stubborn lock still fell across his forehead. His face was freshly shaved, and even from this distance, the fact that he'd rather be anywhere else was easy to read.

She loved that he'd dressed up anyway.

As if sensing her presence, he turned. His eyes found her across the square.

And the world stopped.

She watched his entire body go still, his chest froze mid-breath. His eyes widened, then darkened, tracking from her face down the length of the dress and back up again in a slow perusal that was almost as real as a physical touch. His lips parted slightly. His Adam's apple bobbed as he tried, repeatedly, to swallow.

Then he started walking toward her, and the crowd seemed to melt away, conversations fading to white noise as his long strides ate up the distance between them.

"Ava." Her name on his lips sounded like a prayer and a curse all at once.

"Hi." It came out breathier than she intended. "You clean up nice."

"You clean up..." He stopped, shook his head, and seemed to struggle for words. Liam McGregor, the man who could debate the merits of different wood stains for twenty minutes, was speechless. "I mean. You look..."

"Different?"

"Stunning." The word was rough, honest, and sent heat spiraling through her belly. His eyes dropped to her shoulders, lingered on the bare skin there.

"Do you like the dress? Mama C loaned it to me."

Surprise flashed across his face, and then a softness that made her chest ache. "Beatrice would've loved seeing you in it." He stepped closer, and she caught the scent of pine and leather that made her want to lean in. "You've been working too hard. Your shoulders are tan."

"Three weeks of demolition will do that." She touched his arm, the muscle flexing beneath the cotton. "You feel tense. Crowds not your thing?"

"Not particularly." But he hadn't moved away from her touch. If anything, he'd leaned into it. "Though it's getting better."

"Liam McGregor! About time you showed up!" Mrs Gable's voice cut through the moment like a well-aimed hatchet. The elderly woman bustled over, her eyes twinkling with undisguised glee as they bounced between Ava and Liam. "And you brought our city girl. Don't you two look lovely together."

"Mrs Gable." Liam's voice held a warning that the woman completely ignored.

"That's a nice dress!" Mrs Gable circled Ava with the assessing eye of a general inspecting troops. "Fits you well. You've got curves, dear. Should show them off more often." She patted Liam's arm with a conspiratorial wink. "Don't you think, Liam?"

"I...need a beer," he stuttered, his ears turning red.

"Old Silas is over by the gazebo telling anyone who'll listen that he knew you two would end up together the moment he saw you two at work in that cottage." Mrs Gable was clearly enjoying herself. "We've got a betting pool going on when you'll make it official."

"Mrs Gable" Ava started, mortified.

"I've got my money on Halloween." She sailed off toward the dessert table, leaving them in her wake.

Ava covered her face with her hands. "I'm so sorry. I can leave if this is..."

"Don't." Liam's hand wrapped around her wrist, gently pulling her hands down. His eyes were intense, serious. "Don't leave. Let them talk." His thumb stroked over her pulse point, and she wondered if he could feel how hard her heart was racing. "I don't care what they say."

"You don't?"

"I care that you're here." He said it simply, like it was the most obvious thing in the world. "The rest is just noise."

The band started playing, a slow country-folk melody that drifted across the square like honey. Couples began moving toward the open space in front of the gazebo, swaying together in the fairy light glow. Liam's eyes dropped to the makeshift dance floor, then back to her. He swallowed and seemed to take a big breath. "Dance with me." It wasn't quite a question.

"I didn't think of you as a dancer."

"I'm not." He held out his hand, rough and calloused and steady. "But I'm making an exception."

Her hand slipped into his like it belonged there, like they'd done this a thousand times before. His palm was warm and work-roughened against her softer skin, the contrast sending shivers up her arm. He led her onto the dance floor with a confidence that surprised her, one hand settling at her waist while the other cradled her hand against his chest.

This was different from the cottage.

In the cottage, they'd touched out of necessity, his hands steadying her on a ladder, both of them gripping opposite ends of a beam, standing close while pointing out details on the blueprints. Those touches had been functional, practical, accidental even and easy to dismiss as just part of the work. Or they'd touched with intent, but never for long, like they were exploring each other's personal boundaries, but keeping a respectful distance.

This was intentional and prolonged. Different.

His hand at her waist was deliberate, his fingers spreading slightly to span as much of her as possible. She could feel the heat of his palm through the thin fabric, feel each individual fingertip pressing gently into her side. Their clasped hands rested against his chest, and she could feel his heartbeat, strong and fast, against her knuckles. It was almost as loud as her own.

They fit together perfectly. Her head reached just to his shoulder, the perfect height to rest against if she wanted. His broad chest was a wall of warmth mere inches away, and when he pulled her closer, her soft curves yielded against his harder planes in a way that was both new and inevitable.

"You're tense," he murmured, his breath stirring her hair.

"So are you." Her breath caught in her throat.

"Yeah." He guided them into a gentle sway, his movements surprisingly graceful for a man built like a linebacker. "But for different reasons now."

She tilted her head back to look at him. "What reasons?"

His eyes dropped to her mouth, then back up. "If you don't know, I'm doing something wrong."

Heat flooded her face, her neck, spreading down into her chest. Around them, other couples swayed, and she was distantly aware of eyes on them, the town watching its favorite son dance with the city girl who'd invaded their sanctuary. But Liam's gaze never wavered from her face, his attention so completely focused on her that the rest of the world faded to watercolors.

"What did you want to be when you were a kid?" She asked it partly to break the tension, partly because she desperately wanted to know everything about him.

He blinked, surprised by the shift. "What?"

"When you were little. What did you dream about becoming?"

He was quiet for a moment, guiding them in a slow circle. "A forest ranger. I wanted to spend all day in the woods, away from people, just me and the trees." A small smile tugged at his lips. "Seemed perfect."

"Why didn't you?"

"Granddad Thomas, was practically a father to me since my father left. Instilled in me the love of working with wood and over time I liked the idea of creating and rebuilding this town, piece by piece. I never wanted to leave Willow Creek. Still don't."

The admission hung between them, heavy with implication. Officially, she was still leaving. Intentions and utterances of not wanting to were reaching the end of their sell-by-date and she'd need to officially declare her next move. They both knew it. Neither wanted to say it out loud.

"What about you?" His voice pulled her from the spiral of her thoughts. "What did little Ava want to be?"

"An artist." The answer came without thinking, bypassing all the careful filters she usually kept in place. "I wanted to paint. Silly, right?"

"Why is that silly?"

"Because artists don't make Vice President by thirty-five," she said, in a perfect imitation of her mother. She tried to make it light, joking, but it came out brittle. "Artists don't build successful careers or financial security or..."

"Artists create beauty." He interrupted her carefully constructed rationalization. "They make things that matter to people, things that last." His hand at her waist squeezed gently. "Kind of like renovating old cottages."

She laughed.

"You've been happy." He said it with such quiet certainty that she couldn't dismiss it. "These past three weeks. Covered in dust and swearing at plumbing and learning how to use a miter saw. I've watched you, Ava. You light up when you're creating something."

"I light up when I close a deal too." But even as she said it, she knew it was a lie. Or at least, not the whole truth.

"Do you?" His eyes searched hers. "Or do you just feel relieved that it's over?"

She opened her mouth to argue, but it was very hard to do when she knew it was true. Liam had got to know her well, or had an ability to see into her soul. God help her. Every successful deal, every promotion, every victory in the corporate arena had brought satisfaction, yes, but not joy. Not this bone-deep contentment that came from watching sunlight stream through windows she'd helped install, from running her hands over shelves she'd sanded smooth, from standing back and seeing beauty where there had been decay. From being there with...him.

"I never wanted to stay anywhere," she whispered, the confession pulled from somewhere deep and honest. "Until I came here." She paused, gathering her courage. This is it, cards on the table: "Until I met you."

She tried to deliver it lightly, with a laugh that would give her plausible deniability if he didn't feel the same. But it came out raw and real. She was standing there, exposed and vulnerable. Emotionally naked and with nowhere to hide.

His eyes darkened in response. Was that a pause? "Ava—"

The folk band finished the piece they were playing and decided to follow it with a frenetic fiddle tune. The notes were jagged and bright as they bounced off the hills. Numerous young couples flooded the dancefloor and suddenly the quiet little world that was just Liam and Ava was swamped with noise and energy. She hated crowds and now she was engulfed. Already feeling vulnerable with her confession to Liam, and cloaked in the fear of possible rejection, this sensory input was suddenly overwhelming like a wave that had come crashing through a freshly opened door.

And Liam still hadn't responded.

The vibration of the base made her feet and legs tingle unpleasantly. It was too much. The scent of woodsmoke from the nearby pit-BBQ cloyed at her throat, mixing with the heavy, sweet perfume of late-summer jasmine and the underlying tang of spilled beer.

"Ava I..." Liam started again, but he had to raise his voice to be heard, and thought against it as he cut himself off.

She stepped away, to the edge of the crowd, fighting to get through the throng of people. Her shoulder blades hit the rough bark of a cedar tree. To her left, Mrs Gable was gesturing wildly while telling a story, her laughter a sharp, rhythmic bark that seemed to pierce right through Ava's temples. To her right, a group of teenagers were chasing each other, their shrieks cutting through the music. She was suddenly very aware of the eyes of the townspeople, the curious side-glances, the knowing nods, the silent questioning of the "City Girl" in the silk dress. She was being examined like a specimen under a microscope.

What was happening? She came from the city, where big noise and lots of people were the norm. Never this close though. She'd dealt with pressure every day, social pressure, professional. Three weeks in the country and she couldn't hack some people looking at her?

Or was this because she had dared be honest about wanting to stay with Liam? And he had paused, hadn't he? Oh God! She couldn't take it back! And the house wasn't even finished. She'd have to see him tomorrow!

Ava's hand went to the hollow of her throat. Her pulse was a frantic bird trapped against her skin. The festive lights began to blur into long, dizzying streaks of gold. She tried to take a deep breath, but the air was thick, humid, and crowded with the voices of a hundred people who knew everything about each other and nothing about her.

The music swelled, the fiddle reaching a screeching crescendo, and the world seemed to tilt.

Then, a shadow fell over her.

A large, calloused hand settled firmly on the small of her back. The heat of it soaked through the silk of her dress, a sudden, grounding weight in the middle of the chaos.

"The creek is two minutes that way," Liam's voice was a low, steady rumble near her ear, bypassing the noise of the band. "And it's dead quiet."

Ava didn't look at the crowd. She didn't look at the lights. She just looked at the dark space between the trees where Liam was pointing, and for the first time in what felt like an hour, her lungs finally expanded.

Liam led her away from the golden dome of the festival lights, his hand never leaving the small of her back. With every step, the roar of the fiddle faded, replaced by the soft *crunch-crunch* of dried pine needles and the distant, rhythmic shush of the water. They stepped onto a small wooden footbridge that arched over Willow Creek. Here, the air was ten degrees cooler, smelling sharply of wet stone and moss. The only light came from a sliver of moon reflecting off the black water, casting the world in shades of silver and deep velvet blue.

Ava leaned against the railing, her shoulders finally dropping. The silence wasn't empty; it was heavy and intentional. Her heartbeat was starting to settle again, her breathing returning to normal. The sense of panic that had filled her senses at the town square now at an end.

"Better?" Liam asked. He was standing close, close enough that she could feel the heat radiating off his chest, a stark contrast to the cool mountain mist clinging to her skin.

"I didn't realize how loud it was," she said, with a faint and false smile. Her voice sounded thin and fragile in the vastness of the forest. She took a deep, cleansing breath. "I spend my life in a city of millions, and I've never felt as crowded as I did on that dance floor."

"Small towns have a way of shrinking the air," Liam said. He turned to face her, his silhouette blocking out the rest of the world. He rested his arms on the railing on either side of her, effectively caging her in, though he didn't touch her. "People here... they see a new light in the window and they want to know what it's burning for."

Ava looked up at him. Without the harsh glare of the town square lights, his features were softened by the shadows, making the usual hardness of his jaw look like something carved from the very basalt cliffs surrounding them. The arms, the quiet, this was her chance. Dare she try again? She took a breath. The world paused: "And what are you burning for, Liam?"

The question hung between them, shimmering like the moonlight on the ripples below. Liam didn't answer with words. He reached out, his thumb tracing the line of her cheek, his skin rough, earthy, and impossibly warm.

The "specimen" feeling was gone. She wasn't a city girl under a microscope anymore, she was just a woman on a bridge, held steady by a man who looked at her like she was the only thing in the woods worth seeing.

"I think you know," he murmured, his voice dropping into that low, gravelly register that made the "frantic bird" in her chest start to flutter all over again, but this time, for an entirely different reason.

"We're not just flipping a house any more, are we?" Her voice was barely a whisper.

"No." He whispered it with absolute certainty. "We're not."

He didn't wait for her to bridge the distance. He moved with the slow, deliberate confidence of a man who knew exactly what he wanted. When his hand finally cupped her cheek, the contrast was a jolt to her system. His palm was a map of hard work and yet his touch was incredibly light, as if he were handling something fragile that he had no intention of breaking.

Ava leaned into the heat of him, her breath hitching. She reached up, her fingers tangling in the fabric of his shirt, pulling him closer until the scent of cedar, cool rain, and something purely *Liam* filled her senses.

Then his mouth was on hers.

It wasn't the polite, measured kiss of the men she knew in Chicago. It was a landslide. It was the taste of the mountain, wild, deep, and honest. He kissed her like he'd been holding his breath since the day she'd pulled her car into the gravel driveway.

Ava's world narrowed to the friction of her silk dress against his heavy denim, the cool night air on her skin, and the devastating heat of his tongue. The "City Girl" who always had a five-year plan and a backup exit strategy vanished. There was no promotion, no 30 day deadline, and no board of directors. There was only the low groan of the wooden bridge beneath them and the man who was currently rewriting every rule she had ever lived by.

He pulled back just an inch, his forehead resting against hers, both of them breathing hard. The creek rushed beneath them, indifferent to the fact that the earth had just shifted on its axis.

"That wasn't in the contract," she whispered against his lips, her voice ragged.

Liam let out a breath that was half-laugh, half-growl, his grip tightening on her waist. "The contract is for the house, Ava. That was for us."

The Rhythm of the Hearth

Ava woke to sunlight streaming through the lace curtains, and for the first time in longer than she could remember, her first conscious thought wasn't about what she'd lost. It was about what might be beginning. She reached for her phone on the nightstand, smiling before she even saw Maya's message waiting for her.

"Girl. DETAILS. How was the dance? What happened with Hot Handyman?"

Ava's fingers hovered over the keyboard, her smile deepening as she remembered the warmth of Liam's hand on her waist, the way he'd looked at her under the string lights like she was something precious he'd just discovered. The electricity of that kiss! He had walked her to her car, since walking home was completely unreasonable, but like the gentleman he was, he had bid her goodnight without pushing the boundaries any further. It had been the perfect moment, and neither of them, she assumed, wanted to spoil such a fairytale.

She typed in her phone: "Nothing happened. But the electricity... God, Maya. My whole body was tingling."

"Nothing happened YET. I'm calling that progress. Don't overthink it!"

Ava set the phone down and stretched, feeling the pleasant ache in her muscles from yesterday's work and last night's dancing. The house was quiet around her, but it wasn't the hollow silence that had greeted her that first morning. This quiet was full, alive, like the house itself was holding its breath in anticipation.

She pulled on her work jeans and one of the soft flannel shirts she'd bought herself at a recent trip to Miller's Hardware. While she loved Liam's yellow, she had decided she needed more than one thing to wear. It was a deep green plaid that Maya would definitely not approve of. She padded downstairs in her socks.

The sound of the coffee maker greeted her before she reached the kitchen, and her heart did a small flip when she saw Liam standing by the window, two mugs already set out on the newly refinished counter. He wasn't hammering or measuring or fixing anything. He was just... there. Waiting for her.

"Morning," he said, turning with a smile that made her knees weak. His hair was still damp from a shower, and he was wearing a clean henley that made his shoulders look impossibly broad. He also chose green today.

"Morning." The word came out softer than she'd intended, almost shy.

He poured coffee into both mugs. "I, uh, stopped by Mama C's before I came over." He gestured to a white box on the counter. "Thought you might want some breakfast."

Ava lifted the lid to find two still-warm croissants and what looked like Mama C's famous cinnamon rolls. Her throat tightened with an emotion she couldn't quite name. "You brought me pastries."

"Don't make it weird." But his ears had gone pink, and he couldn't quite meet her eyes.

"Too late. It's already weird." She picked up a croissant and took a bite, closing her eyes as the buttery layers melted on her tongue. When she opened them again, Liam was watching her with an expression that made heat pool low in her belly. "What?"

"Nothing." He shook his head, a smile playing at the corners of his mouth. "You look different this morning."

"Different how?"

"Happy."

The word hung between them, simple and true. Ava realized with a start that she was happy. Not the manic, prove-something-to-everyone happiness she'd chased in Chicago. This was quieter, deeper, like a seed that had finally found the right soil to take root.

"Yeah," she said softly. "I guess I am."

They stood there for a moment, coffee mugs warming their hands, the rich sugary goodness of Mama C's food coursing through their veins, the morning light painting everything gold. When Liam reached past her for the sugar, his arm brushed hers, and instead of moving away, they both lingered. His skin was warm through the thin fabric of her shirt, and she could smell his soap, and something crisp that made her want to lean closer.

"So," Liam said, his voice rougher than usual. "Ready for another day of grunt work?"

Ava glanced at her thirty-day schedule posted on the refrigerator, the one she'd made with such militant precision that first week. She'd crossed off tasks with angry slashes at first, each X a countdown to escape. But somewhere along the way, her crosses had become checkmarks, and she'd started adding notes in the margins: *Liam showed me how to sand with the grain. Mama C brought soup. Silas told me about Beatrice's garden.*

According to the schedule, she was actually ahead of time. The thought should have filled her with relief, instead she was compressed by a feeling close to dread. The schedule reminded her of her Chicago life and an impending deadline to formalise her decision. Of letters of demand from the bank for their balloon payment...

"Ava?" Liam was watching her, concern creasing his brow.

"Yeah," she said quickly, forcing brightness into her voice. "Let's do this."

The work had changed. They weren't tearing things apart anymore, weren't fighting with rusted pipes and crumbling plaster. Today was about the delicate finishing touches, installing the vintage brass hardware Ava had sourced from an antique dealer in Portland, hanging the pantry door they'd spent three days carefully restoring, painting the trim in the warm cream color she'd agonized over for an entire evening.

Ava stood in the living room, surveying the paint samples she'd taped to the wall. A real estate agent would recommend "Agreeable Gray" or "Accessible Beige" safe, marketable colors that would appeal to the broadest range of buyers. But when she looked at those samples, all she saw was Beatrice's house stripped of its soul, turned into just another property listing.

"What about this one?" Liam appeared beside her, pointing to a sample she'd almost dismissed. "The 'Buttercream'?"

Ava tilted her head, studying it. It was warmer than the grays, richer than the beiges. It reminded her of the way morning light looked filtering through the kitchen windows. She smiled. "It's not very modern."

"Neither is the house." Liam crossed his arms, his shoulder just touching hers. "You spent all this time bringing back the original woodwork, refinishing the floors to show the old growth patterns. Why would you paint over all that character with something that looks like every other flipped house in America?"

She looked at him, and teasingly said "I thought you'd want to leave all the walls a bare wood to show off the natural beauty."

"I thought I would too." He met her gaze, and something in his expression made her breath catch. "But I've been wrong about a lot of things."

They stood close enough that she could practically feel his heartbeat. The air between them charged, electric with possibility.

"Buttercream it is," she said softly.

His smile was like the sunrise. "Good choice."

They fell into a rhythm almost like a dance. Ava would climb the ladder to cut in the ceiling edges, and Liam would hand her the brush before she had to ask. When she needed the paint tray repositioned, he was already moving it. They worked in comfortable silence punctuated by occasional laughter, their movements synchronized in a way that was effortless and right.

"Hand me the level?" Liam was installing the last piece of crown molding, balanced on a stepladder.

Ava grabbed it from the toolbox and moved to pass it up to him. As she reached, she deliberately leaned in closer than necessary, letting their bodies touch, feeling his strong solid frame against her breast. She heard the sharp intake of his breath and smiled to herself.

"Thank you," he said hoarsely. He marked something with a pencil and climbed down from the ladder, moving slowly, deliberately, until he was standing close enough that she had to tilt her head back to maintain eye contact. Now his turn to test her boundary.

For a breathless moment, she thought he might kiss her right there, paint-spattered and dusty in the middle of the half-finished living room. But instead, he reached up and tucked a strand of hair behind her ear, his fingers lingering against her cheek.

"We should probably finish this room before Silas shows up," he said, his voice low.

"Probably," she agreed, not moving. The teasing was delicious and agony all at the same time.

They stood there for another heartbeat, then two, before Liam finally stepped back with visible effort. But his eyes never left hers, and the promise in them made her knees weak.

They returned to work, the air between them heavy with possibility, sweet with anticipation. Every accidental touch sent sparks through her nervous system. When their fingers brushed reaching for the same paintbrush, neither pulled away quickly. When Liam steadied the ladder and his hand landed on the small of her back, the warmth of it penetrated all the way through her entire body.

This, she thought, was more intimate than the dance. This quiet harmony, this physical awareness of each other, this sense of being so perfectly in sync that words became unnecessary. It was terrifying and exhilarating and absolutely right.

They were taking a break on the front porch, sharing a sleeve of Oreos Liam had produced from his truck, when Silas's mail van pulled up to the curb.

"Special delivery!" The mailman climbed out with a large box in his arms and his perpetual smile firmly in place. "Looks like Christmas came early for the new girl."

Ava jumped up to help him, recognizing the return address. "It's the light fixture! I was starting to think it got lost."

"Not on my watch." Silas set the box down carefully and then stood back, hands on his hips, surveying the house with an appraising eye. "Well, would you look at that. The old place is breathing again."

It was such an odd way to phrase it that it gave Ava pause. But when she followed his gaze, she understood what he meant. The house did look alive now, the fresh paint gleaming in the afternoon sun, the repaired porch welcoming instead of treacherous, the windows no longer blank and dead but reflecting the sky and trees like open eyes.

"Beatrice would be proud," Silas continued, his voice going soft. "Real proud of what you've done here. Both of you."

"We still have work to do," Ava said, but warmth bloomed in her chest at his words.

"Maybe. But you brought back its soul. That's what matters." Silas pulled an envelope from his bag, this one yellowed with age. "Speaking of Beatrice, I, uh, found this in the back of my mailbag this morning. She left it with me a few months before she passed, with special instructions on when to give it to you. Seeing the house now...I think it's time."

Ava took the letter with trembling fingers. Beatrice's handwriting was shakier than in the earlier letters, but still recognizable.

"She was always writing letters," Silas said, tipping his hat to them both. He took a few steps towards the van and turned. "Whole town's talking, you know. About the new girl who came to flip a house and ended up saving it instead." His eyes twinkled as he looked between Ava and Liam. "They're all rooting for you to stick around. Both of you."

After he left, Ava stood holding the letter, afraid to open it. What if this one said something different? What if Beatrice had regrets at the end?

"Want me to give you a minute?" Liam asked gently.

"No." She sat down on the porch steps, and he settled beside her, close enough that their shoulders touched. She carefully opened the envelope.

My dearest Ava,

If you're reading this, you've made it further than I dared hope. You've brought a new life back to my old home, and no doubt discovered many of its secrets along the way. If you did the kitchen properly, you will have seen my collection, and know my story. You understand that this house holds more than rooms and rafters, it holds a life lived on my own terms.

I won't lie to you. There were days I wondered what might have been if I'd chosen differently at various times. If I'd made the decision to defy my family, or if I'd made a later one to move away or move on and find love again. But while not perfect, I had a good life, and a special, very dear friendship that lasted many years. I made a decision to stay in Willow Creek and nurture that friendship and I am rewarded every time I bake bread, or walk through my garden, or sit in my nook to watch the afternoon sun. I am happy.

The world will tell you what to value. Money, status, other people's approval. They'll convince you that playing it safe is the same as being happy. They'll make you believe that loving something, or someone, that doesn't fit their script is foolish.

Don't listen.

Choose your heart, and never once regret it. It's never too late. This house, this life, this beautiful, messy, imperfect existence, it was mine. Wholly, completely mine.

Whatever you're facing, whatever choice looms before you, remember this: regret doesn't come from following your heart. It comes from denying it.

Choose the life that makes you feel most alive, even if it scares you.
Especially if it scares you.
With hope, Beatrice

Ava's vision blurred with tears. Liam's hand covered hers, warm and steady and real.

"She was right," Ava whispered. "About all of it."

"Yeah," Liam said. "She was."

They sat in silence as the afternoon light turned golden, the letter resting in Ava's lap. She thought about all the choices that had led her here, the job she hated, loans she couldn't afford, the inheritance she'd viewed as an inconvenient burden. At the time, each had felt like a failure, a wrong turn, a door slamming shut. But maybe they'd all been leading her here. To this house. To this moment. To this man sitting beside her whose presence was now as essential as breathing.

"I was wrong about you," Liam said suddenly.

Ava turned to look at him, her heart hammering. "What?"

"When you first got here, I thought you were just another outsider looking to make a quick buck. Another person who'd see dollar signs instead of history, who'd gut this place and slap on some subway tile and call it progress." He met her gaze, and the vulnerability in his eyes made her chest ache. "But you didn't just flip this house, Ava. You saved it. You honored it. You made it beautiful again without erasing what made it special."

She started to speak, but he cut her off.

"I'm not done." He shifted to face her more fully, his pulse making his neck jump. "These past few weeks, working with you, watching you fall in love with this place and this town... It's been the best time I've had in years. Maybe ever. And I don't want it to end."

The world seemed to narrow to just the two of them, sitting on the porch of a house that had been rebuilt with their own hands. Ava's schedule said she had five days until she was supposed to pack up and leave, put the house on the market, and return to Chicago to stave off financial disaster and rebuild her old life. But sitting here with Liam's hand warm on hers, with Beatrice's words echoing in her mind, with the house breathing peacefully around them, the thought of leaving was like tearing herself in half.

"I don't want it to end either," she admitted, her voice barely above a whisper.

The look Liam gave her was so full of hope and heat and tenderness that she couldn't breathe. For the first time in a long time, Ava's chorus of inner doubt and conflict were silent.

An Unwanted Guest

Liam had left to go to town to pick up a few things from Miller's Hardware and promised to get something for dinner for the two of them to have that night. Steaks. They'd planned it that afternoon, a celebration meal for finishing the porch, for crossing another milestone. That was the 'official' reason, but Ava thought of it more, and hoped Liam did too, as a celebration for coming together as something else. Liam was going to grill them while Ava made the salad, and they'd eat on the newly completed porch and watch the stars come out. Simple. Perfect. Theirs.

Ava was sweeping up and generally tidying, but her mind was already thinking ahead, planning next steps. Not with the house of course, but with Liam. For a woman whose entire career was built on Five-Year Plans and market projections, the future had suddenly stopped looking like a spreadsheet and started looking like a home. As Ava polished the last of the dust from the fireplace mantle, she was already mentally rearranging the guest room into a nursery, white-oak cribs and soft, forest-green textiles that would mirror the trees outside the window. She could see it all with terrifying clarity: an "Oasis" bistro set finally laid out for summer breakfasts, Liam's heavy boots drying by the door for the next twenty years, and the two of them growing old as the Willow tree roots claimed the yard.

Tonight was the beginning of that "forever". She had already mentally made a promise not to eat too much of the steak. She had picked out her favorite silk slip, the one that was a quiet invitation, and tucked a bottle of wine in the back of the fridge. She was giddy, her heart performing a restless, rhythmic dance against her ribs as she imagined the weight of his hand on her waist without the barrier of a dance floor or a bridge between them. She was building a castle in the air, brick by happy brick, convinced that for the first time in her life, she had finally found a foundation that couldn't be shaken.

She was smiling to herself with happy thoughts, when a voice burst her bubble.

"Well, well. Isn't this cozy."

Ava froze, a reptilian response honed from years of hearing that voice. Her mood, her happy thoughts and future plans, all drained from her mind like the voice had pulled a plug somewhere near her feet. Her breath froze in her chest.

A man stood at the front door, casting a shadow over her perfectly restored floors and the future she was dreaming of making there.

Martin.

He looked exactly the same, charcoal suit perfectly tailored, hair with a touch of salt and pepper around the temples, artfully styled, Italian leather shoes that probably cost more than all the lumber she and Liam had used to rebuild the kitchen. He straightened his cuffs with practiced precision, his movements unhurried and confident, with a smile that didn't quite reach his eyes. The cottage, the mountain evening, the small-town setting, none of it touched him. He wore his urban polish like armor, completely impervious to the rustic charm surrounding him.

Ava stared at her boss and ex-lover, frozen to the spot. Though no time had passed, this horrible moment had already lasted an eternity. His gaze was cataloging everything, the floor, the walls, the paint on her jeans, her messy hair, the new found musculature in her arms. She shuddered to think what he was doing with that image in his mind, and was mildly sick remembering he knew what she looked like naked.

"Hello, Ava," Martin said smoothly. "Surprise."

The house seemed to hold its breath, waiting.

"Martin." She struggled to get her voice to come out steady without betraying the warring emotions inside of her. "What are you doing here?"

"We need to talk. Privately, if you're alone?"

Ava's mind raced. She could send Martin away, tell him to leave her alone on this perfect evening she was preparing for with a man she wanted to spend time with. But she knew Martin. He'd flown all the way from Chicago, because phone calls and emails hadn't worked. Telling him to wait hadn't worked. He wouldn't leave without answers, and the conversation that needed to happen would poison whatever was blooming between her and Liam if it hung over her unresolved.

She needed to close this door before she could walk through a new one.

Martin raised his eyebrows as if to ask "are we alone?"

"Yes, I'm alone. My...contractor has gone to get some supplies" she said.

"Can I come in then?" Martin asked with a laugh, already moving inside. She could smell his expensive cologne, something deep and musky he always wore. It announced his presence before he arrived and lingered afterwards to remind you he was there. It was perfect in a Chicago office. It was just wrong out here. Not the man to wait for invitations when he could just take something, he very smoothly transitioned into sales mode. "This place looks great! You could sell it for a mint. Buy quite a nice condo in the West Loop. Is that molding original..."

Ava was still trying to come up to speed with what was happening and was only following along with Martin's spiel with half an ear. She was acutely aware of how out of place he looked against the backdrop of the cottage she'd poured her heart into. His expensive shoes clicked against the refinished floorboards she'd sanded on her hands and knees. His manicured hands touched the railing she and Liam had built together, and she had to suppress the urge to tell him not to.

The cottage was different with Martin in it. Smaller. Less like home and more like a stage set, something pretty but ultimately temporary. She watched him take in the exposed beams, the restored fireplace, the original woodwork she'd fought so hard to preserve, and saw only dismissal in his expression despite the praise in his words.

"It's charming," he finished, in the same tone he might use for a child's art project. "Very... rustic."

He set his leather briefcase on the kitchen island, a butcher block surface she'd spent three days conditioning and oiling until it glowed, and brushed an invisible speck of dust from his sleeve. The gesture was small but telling. This place, this life she'd been building, was beneath him. A quaint hobby. A phase to be indulged and then abandoned.

Ava hardened. "You came 2,000 miles to critique my decorating choices?" she asked.

"I came 2,000 miles because you've been avoiding my calls." Martin opened his briefcase with practiced efficiency, pulling out a manila folder that looked ominously official. "And because this couldn't wait any longer. Derek's out."

The words hung in the air between them. Ava's breath caught in her throat. "What?"

"Derek Morrison. You remember him. Golden boy who took your promotion from you." Martin's smile was sharp, satisfied. "Turns out he was padding his expense reports and taking kickbacks from vendors. The board found out last week. He's been terminated."

Ava's mind reeled. Derek, smug, untouchable Derek who'd charmed the partners and stolen her promotion, was gone. The news should have filled her with vindication, with the sweet taste of justice served. Instead, she had an odd hollow feeling inside, like a void sucking up any positive emotion to the news.

Martin continued, warming to his pitch. "Which means the Creative Director position is open again. And the board agrees that it should have been yours from the beginning. Especially now we've...tidied up that misunderstanding between us." He slid a document across the island toward her. "Thirty percent raise. Signing bonus of $50,000. Your own team. Corner office. Everything we discussed before."

Ava stared at the contract without touching it. It sat there, taking up the entire room and sucking oxygen from air around her. The numbers were impressive, more money than she'd ever thought she'd make, a bonus that would clean out that personal loan, and without those payments she'd have more than enough to start quickly chipping away her student loans. And better, with that base salary she could get out of the studio and afford a luxury apartment she'd always wanted. A condo in Streeterville maybe? High-rise. Doorman. A sleek glass-walled piece of heaven overlooking the Lake. It would be like living in an architectural magazine.

And the title. The title was everything she'd worked toward for six years. With that title she would have respect, sitting in her corner office. Rumours would surely be a thing of the past if she was the boss. She'd get her life back and under control. It was everything she'd ever wanted. Four weeks ago.

"There's more." Martin's voice took on that particular timbre he used when closing a deal, when he sensed weakness and moved in for the kill. "The board has authorized me to make you an additional offer." He pulled out a second set of papers. "Midwest Properties LLC, one of our holding companies, is looking to acquire historical properties for renovation and resale. They're prepared to pay fifteen percent over market value for this cottage. We can have the papers signed tonight and you back in Chicago by Monday."

The room seemed to tilt.

"You want to buy the cottage?" Ava said slowly.

"We want to make your transition back to real life as easy as possible." Martin's tone was reasonable, logical. "You've had your time away, Ava. You've done your grieving, your soul-searching, whatever...this was. And it's been good for you, I can see that. You look healthier, more relaxed. But you're a shark, and sharks don't belong in ponds this small.

You've got real talent, not just for architecture but in the board room, with clients, making big deals and having big ideas. We need you back."

The casual dismissal of everything she'd built here made her hands curl into fists. This wasn't a pond. This was Willow Creek, where Mama C knew how everyone took their coffee and Silas delivered mail with a side of local gossip, and Sophie organized the book clubs that will welcome you like family. This was the place where she'd learned that success could be measured in refinished floorboards and hand-sanded banisters. Where she'd discovered that the most valuable things couldn't be quantified in spreadsheets or quarterly reports.

"Hang on," she said, catching up to the conversation. "When you called the other night, you offered me Partner, but didn't mention anything about Creative Director. But the Board has known about Derek and his finances for a week, you said. What are you playing at?"

Martin gave a small sigh. "To be honest Ava, it took me a lot to convince the Board to give you this position. They wanted to put Creative Director back out there." He chose his next words carefully, "the little...misunderstanding between us didn't...endear you to the Board members. I mean, no one wants a living HR issue walking around in a position at the top. But I've spent the better part of the last week singing your praises and convincing them they ought to just cut out the middle man and offer it right to you. Once I explained how HR investigated and found it was all a misunderstanding and how there is no animosity or any "bunny boiling" tendencies inside of you, they...they came round. I vouched for you personally, because I knew you wouldn't let me down. I mean, Partner was, is, yours anyway. Six years of great work. It's about time isn't it? I was just ringing the other night to give you that good news. Thought it would make you happy! But Creative Director, this is big. This is control over not just the Lincoln Park deal, this is everything."

Ava was almost physically ill. 'Little misunderstanding' kept playing in her mind. "You told everyone I was sleeping my way to the top," she said. "No one would come near me for weeks, months! That's not a little 'misunderstanding' Martin, that was stone cold murder of my reputation."

"I know," he said quietly, and bowed his head. "And I'm sorry. The truth is, I had real feelings for you Ava. I still do. I know the affair was wrong, and unfair to my wife, but I screwed up and was hurt when you called it off. I was immature and took it out on you, and I shouldn't have. I'm sorry."

Ava had known Martin for a long time. Heard him apologise a thousand times, for overruns, for blowouts, for other people's mistakes. She knew when he was being insincere, could read it in his voice and body language a mile off. This time...he seemed genuine.

Seeing the hesitation in her eyes, no doubt, he leaned forward, his expression earnest in the way he got when he really wanted something. "You've proved your point, whatever it was. You can fix things with your hands, you can survive without your corporate salary, you're more than just an executive. Congratulations. You've punished me, and punished the firm for a month, and we suffered for it, we really did. But now it's time to come home. Time to taste the reward for all your efforts, make some money, live the good life. Really achieve something, design buildings that will last a hundred years. Time to use that brilliant mind on projects that actually matter, that impact thousands of people instead of just one dusty cottage."

"This cottage isn't dusty," Ava said, her voice sharp. "And the work we've done here does matter."

"We?" Martin's eyebrow arched. "You mean you and the local handyman? Ava, be serious. This isn't a future, it's a fantasy. What are you going to do, play house in the mountains? Spend your days picking wildflowers and having deep conversations about wood grain? I bet they don't even have a good Caramel Macchiato in this place. Do they even do real coffee?"

The mockery in his voice ignited something fierce in her chest. Yes, she wanted to say. Yes, that's exactly what I want to do. Because those conversations about wood grain had taught her more about patience and craftsmanship and beauty than any board meeting ever had. Because picking wildflowers with Liam had made her happier than closing million-dollar deals. And, damn it, Mama C's coffee was better than Starbucks. She wanted to say that she'd rather have calluses on her hands and sawdust in her hair than spend another day in meetings that accomplished nothing, working for people who saw her as a tool rather than a person.

But the words stuck in her throat, tangled up with fear and doubt and the weight of six years of building a life and the prospect of finally getting the reward for all that work, versus throwing it all away.

Martin softened his tone, reading her hesitation. "I'm not trying to be cruel, Ava. I'm trying to be honest. You're one of the most talented architects I've ever worked with. You're wasted here. And deep down, you know it."

Did she? Weeks ago, she would have agreed instantly. Would have seen this offer as the lifeline she'd been praying for. Now, standing in the kitchen where she and Liam had shared coffee and pastries and easy conversation, where they'd laughed over paint samples and argued about cabinet hardware, where they'd built something real and lasting together, the corporate title was just a trap disguised as a prize.

But the Willow Creek life, the cottage life, the Liam life was also terrifying in its uncertainty. And it certainly didn't address her balloon payment. There was no point staying if she was just going to be hounded by debt collectors or sending every penny she had back to Chicago banks just trying to stave off bankruptcy another week. Martin was offering her security, status, a path she knew how to walk. What did she have here? A mostly-finished house and feelings for a man she'd known less than a month. No guarantees. No five-year plan. Nothing but hope and sawdust and the reckless belief that she could build something lasting. What if her heart was wrong? What if this was just a fantasy, like Martin said? What if she was confusing the thrill of something new with actual love, mistaking a temporary escape for a permanent solution? What if she was on the verge of throwing away six long years for...a fling? The previous thoughts of nurseries and boots by a door for twenty years became thoughts of a relationship over by next summer, and crawling back to Chicago with nothing but a bankruptcy notice.

But what if she could have both, she thought. Take the role in Chicago, the title, the signing bonus, the big salary. Maybe over time she could convince Liam to move? How long? A year? Six months? With her new salary she could afford to visit Willow Creek for long weekends until he was ready to move. Then he could come work for her, oversee large scale construction, making things that will last. It wouldn't be with the wood he's used to, but over time she might be able to make him choose her over carpentry. They'd be together and she'd have everything she'd ever wanted.

Ava moved to the window, looking out at the driveway where Liam's truck had been parked all day. The space was empty now, his absence a physical ache in Ava's chest.

"You're offering me everything I thought I wanted," she said quietly.

"I'm offering you everything you've earned." Martin's reflection appeared in the window beside hers. "Say yes, Ava. Come back where you belong. Let us handle the cottage sale, get you top dollar, more than you'd get on the open market. You could be back in your apartment by next weekend, and buying something grand the weekend after. Back to your real life."

Her real life. The phrase echoed in her mind, hollow and false. Which life was real? The one where she wore designer suits and worked seventy-hour weeks and went to sleep every night feeling empty? Or the one where she woke up excited to sand floors and install crown molding and learn the difference between dovetail joints and mortise-and-tenon?

Ava turned from the window to face Martin. He stood beside the island, confident and polished, holding out the contracts like they were a life raft, one for Creative Director, one to buy the cottage. Behind him, she could see the built-in shelves Liam had restored, the fireplace they'd cleaned together, the floors they'd refinished on their hands and knees.

Every surface held a memory. Every corner whispered of the life she was choosing between.

Her phone buzzed in her pocket. She pulled it out to see a text from Liam: *Butcher was out of ribeye. Got New York strips instead. Hope that's okay.*

Such a simple message. Such a profound promise. He was still planning dinner, still believing they had a future.

Ava looked at the contracts. Then at her phone. Then at the cottage.

"Give me the paperwork," she said.

Martin's smile was triumphant as he slid the contracts across the island toward her. "You're making the right choice, Ava. I promise you won't regret this." He put a hand on her shoulder. Her stomach turned.

Martin headed for the door "I'll leave you to your evening. I'm staying in town overnight, you can drop them off to me in the morning. And Ava?"

"Yes"

"Welcome to the big leagues." And he was gone.

The Blueprint of a Life

The cottage was too quiet.

Ava sat at the kitchen island, her hands wrapped around a mug of coffee that had gone cold an hour ago. She should call Maya. Her best friend would know what to say, would help her sort through the tangle of thoughts that had been spinning in her head since Martin's departure. Maya, who understood the language of corner offices and career trajectories, who'd watched Ava build herself back up piece by careful piece every time Chicago threw something new at her.

But when Ava reached for her phone, her fingers stopped halfway. Because Maya would ask the logical questions, about salary, about opportunities, about leveraging her position. Maya would remind her of the handbags they'd coveted together in shop windows, the shoes that cost a month's rent, the life they'd both aspired to when they were 22 and hungry and certain that success could be measured in square footage and thread count. Maya would promise fine wine, and brunch, and dining, and social scenes now open to her in her new, well paid role.

Ava thought about handbags now. Tried to summon the old hunger for them. Found only a hollow space where that wanting used to live.

Instead, her mind filled with the weight of solid oak beneath her palms. The satisfying resistance of wood that had grown for a century before she'd ever touched it. The way Liam's hands looked when he worked, scarred and capable, moving with a certainty she'd spent her whole life chasing through conference rooms and client presentations.

She thought about caramel macchiatos from the Starbucks three blocks from her old Chicago office, where baristas she'd never learned the names of made her drink exactly the same way every single morning for five years. Efficient. Consistent. Utterly forgettable. Then she thought about Mama C's diner, where the coffee was too strong and came with unsolicited advice and a warmth that had nothing to do with temperature. Where Mama C knew how she liked her eggs before Ava had ordered once. Where every meal came with a side of community, of being known, of mattering to people who had no professional obligation to remember her name.

The contract sat on the counter, its crisp white pages almost luminous, each of them filled with promise. Promise and forgiveness, especially forgiveness of a lot of debt. Martin had left it behind like a calling card, borne on the scent of his expensive cologne. It was more than everything she'd ever wanted. It was vindication. Proof that she'd been right to sacrifice, to climb, to become the kind of woman who could command a room and close a deal and never, ever let them see her doubt.

She pushed back the stool, letting it scrape against the floor with a sound that echoed too loud in the empty kitchen. She paced back and forth a few times, then moved to the window, and pressed her forehead against the cool glass. Outside, the garden she and Liam had started clearing last week was half-tamed, still wild but beginning to show the bones of something intentional. Something loved. She'd done that. Not delegated it, not managed it from a distance, but actually dug in the dirt with her own hands until her shoulders ached and her nails were ruined and she'd never been more proud of anything in her entire life.

The sound of tires on gravel made her heart lurch. She turned from the window to see Liam's truck pulling into the drive, and something in her chest both tightened and loosened at once.

He was back.

She watched him climb out, moving with that easy economy of motion she'd come to know so well. He reached into the truck bed and pulled out a brown paper bag, and even from here she could make out the butcher shop logo.

Ava's hands were shaking. What would she say? Where would she start? "I've had a great offer" or straight to "come with me to Chicago?"

The front door opened. She heard Liam's boots on the refinished hardwood, heard him pause in the entryway.

When he appeared in the kitchen doorway, something in his expression made her breath catch. The easy warmth from earlier was gone, replaced by something careful and distant that reminded her painfully of those first few days, when he'd looked at her like she was just another outsider with a checkbook and shallow roots. The scent that Martin left behind betrayed the fact she had a visitor, and one that didn't fit in the place. She knew that Liam could read it and knew what it meant before Ava could say a word.

"I got ribeyes," he said, his voice neutral as he set the bag on the counter, his eyes darting around. "Like we talked about."

His eyes found the contract.

She watched him take it in, the corporate letterhead, the dense paragraphs of legalese, Martin's business card paper-clipped to the top.

Ava realised too late, her mistake in not moving them away sooner. Or did her subconscious intend to put this out in the open?

He didn't ask. Didn't reach for it or comment on it or demand an explanation. He just looked at it like it was a snake coiled on her kitchen counter, then deliberately turned his attention back to unpacking the steaks.

The air in the cottage was toxic with Martin's lingering cologne and unspoken questions, and the weight of the choice that sat between them like a third person neither of them wanted to acknowledge.

"Martin, my boss, was here," Ava finally said, her voice coming out rougher than she'd intended.

"Yeah, I figured." Liam pulled out the cutting board with precise movements. "That cologne's quite pungent."

"He told me Derek quit. Well, fired actually. The guy who got my promotion?" The words tasted bitter. "Apparently he was falsifying his expenses. Taking kickbacks. Not a good guy, from the sounds of it." She tried to keep the tone light and informational like she had nothing to hide, which was a lie she kept telling herself.

Liam's jaw tightened, but he didn't look at her. "That's convenient timing."

"That's what I said." Ava's hands clenched into fists. "He came all the way out here, showed up uninvited, just to tell me they 'made a mistake.' Like I'm supposed to be grateful they finally figured out what I've known for years..."

Liam's voice cut through her rising anger, quiet but firm, clearly also trying to keep it light but also betraying his true feelings. "You don't have to explain. Let's just eat."

Ava knew what his tone really meant, it said *I already know how this ends.*

They moved around each other in the kitchen with a terrible, careful courtesy. Liam prepped the steaks while Ava pulled out plates and silverware, both of them maintaining a physical distance that might have well been miles. The easy rhythm they'd found over the past weeks, the casual touches, the comfortable silences, the way they'd learned to anticipate each other's movements, was gone. She didn't know how to start the conversation, to explain the mess that were her thoughts. He didn't even try to ask.

When they finally sat down to eat, the scraping of forks against plates was the only sound in the room. Ava pushed a piece of perfectly cooked steak around her plate, her appetite gone. Across from her, Liam ate with mechanical precision, his eyes fixed on his food like it required his complete concentration.

This was wrong. Everything about this was wrong. This morning they'd laughed over coffee and made plans for the garden. This evening they were strangers again, separated by a piece of paper and all the assumptions neither of them was brave enough to voice.

"The steak's good," she offered quietly.

"Thanks."

Another silence. Longer this time. Suffocating.

Ava watched Liam's hand tighten around his fork, watched the muscle in his cheek pulse. He was holding something back, something that was eating at him from the inside.

"Just ask me," she said.

He looked up then, and the pain in his eyes made her chest ache. "Ask you what?"

"Whatever you're thinking. Whatever you're assuming." She set down her fork. "I can see it on your face, Liam. You're already halfway out the door in your head."

His laugh was hollow, humorless. "That's funny, coming from you."

"What's that supposed to mean?"

"It means I can read, Ava. Creative Director. Nice six figures. Chicago." He gestured toward the contract, still sitting on the counter like an accusation. "It means I always knew this was temporary. I just—" He stopped, shook his head. "I just didn't expect it to hurt this much, or to be so final just sitting there on the kitchen table."

Ava's heart cracked. "You think I've already decided."

"Haven't you?" His voice was quiet, devastatingly gentle. "Be honest. A month ago, you didn't even want to be here. Now they're offering you everything you've worked for. Why would you stay?"

The question hung in the air between them, and Ava realized with a jolt that he genuinely didn't know the answer. Liam, solid and steady, who'd shown her how to sand with the grain and read the history in old wood and find beauty in things everyone else wanted to tear down, didn't believe he was reason enough to stay. She should tell him. Tell him there were options at least. Staying, yes, but the best of both worlds was open to them. He could come too. He could be part of her life, in a Streeterville condo and they could be together and happy.

But could he be happy in Chicago? Liam, who worked with wood and loved this town and its people, had tried the big city once and he had made it clear he never wanted to return. She was naive in ever think-ing that the best of both worlds was going to be a possibility. She would have to choose, it was inevitable.

So, maybe she should reach across this table and take his hand and explain that Chicago was a past life, that the corner office meant nothing compared to the way her heart lifted every morning when she heard his truck in the driveway, that she'd spent the last hour trying to remember why she'd ever wanted those handbags when what she really wanted was this, him, the cottage, the life they were building together.

But the words stuck in her throat, tangled up with indecision and wishful thinking of having it all. Tangled up with hurt and pride and a stubborn anger that he could think she was so easily bought back by the people who'd discarded her the moment she became inconvenient that she would leave him without a second thought. If he doesn't think he's enough, will he stay when times get hard? Will he be around a year from now, two? Will he fight for us, or run at the first sign of trouble? When I'm penniless from loans and debts and stuck out here in the middle of Oregon having given up on my only chance to clear my slate and get ahead, where will he be? Chicago may be cold, and cruel, but it's not go-ing anywhere. But Liam?

"You really think that little of me," she said instead.

Liam's eyes widened. "That's not..."

"You think I'm the kind of person who'd throw away everything we've built here just for a title and a paycheck." Her voice was shaking now. "After everything, after all the work, all the late nights, all the con-versations about what matters and what doesn't, you still see me as the corporate climber who showed up with her suitcase and her exit strategy who would just leave you behind?"

"That's not fair, Ava. I'm trying to be realistic..."

"No, you're trying to protect yourself. You're already grieving this, aren't you? You've already decided I'm leaving, so you're getting ahead of it. Leaving me before I can possibly leave you. Building your walls back up before I can hurt you. Is this how it would be? Always leaving at the first sight of something hard?"

The truth of it hung between them, sharp and painful.

Liam pushed back from the table, standing abruptly. "When does your flight leave?"

The question was a knife between her ribs. "I don't..."

"Because I need to know. I need to know how much time I have to..." He stopped, ran a hand through his hair. "I need to finish the trim work in the master bedroom. And the porch railing still needs another coat of stain. I need to know how much time I have to finish this job."

This job. Was that all it had ever been? Where were his feelings about her? She may have been delusional ever contemplating an idea of Chicago and Liam, but at least Liam was in the picture there. Where was she in his world? Clearly not worth fighting for, clearly just another job. Were the past weeks of working side by side, of stolen glances and almost-kisses and the slow, inevitable fall into something like forever nothing more to him than the punch list?

"Get out," Ava said quietly.

Liam froze. "What?"

"Get out. Go home. I can't..." Her voice cracked. "I can't do this with you right now. I can't sit here and watch you turn back into the stranger who glared at me that first day. I can't."

She couldn't finish. Couldn't put words to the way her heart was breaking, to the fact that she'd been so close to choosing him, choosing this, and now he'd gone and made it about whether he was *enough* instead of about whether this life was right.

Liam stared at her for a long moment, his face a careful mask. Then he nodded once, sharp and final. "As you wish."

He grabbed his jacket from the back of the chair, his movements stiff and controlled. At the doorway, he paused, his back to her.

"For what it's worth," he said, his voice rough, "I never thought you were shallow. I just know I can't compete with the life they're offering you. And I won't ask you to give up your dreams for a guy with sawdust in his hair and a mortgage on a fixer-upper."

The door closed behind him.

Ava stood alone in the kitchen, surrounded by the evidence of the meal they'd never really eaten. The steaks on the plates, barely touched. The contract on the counter, pristine and white and full of promises that suddenly felt hollow.

She listened to his truck start, listened to the crunch of gravel as he pulled away. Listened to the silence that rushed in to fill the space where he'd been.

And burst into tears.

Ava stood in the middle of the kitchen. The silence crashed over her like a wave. The steaks sat congealing on their plates. The contract sat pristine and accusatory on the counter. And she was alone with the biggest decision of her life.

Her phone buzzed. Martin again: Waiting to hear from you. Don't overthink this, Ava. You know what the smart choice is.

The smart choice. She'd built her entire life on smart choices. Strategic choices. Choices that looked good on paper and made sense to everyone around her. And where had that gotten her? Miserable in a studio apartment, overlooked and used by people who valued her productivity but not her humanity, so deep in debt she couldn't see daylight.

This house was supposed to fix all that. Flip it, sell it, use the profit to finally get ahead. Except she hadn't flipped it. She'd fallen in love with it. Fallen in love with the town. Fallen in love with a man who looked at her like she was capable of miracles.

Ava's hands were shaking. She pressed them flat against the butcher block counter, the one she'd spent three days conditioning until it glowed like honey, and tried to breathe.

Think, she commanded herself. Actually think this through.

She grabbed a notepad, the same one where she'd made her initial thirty-day timeline, now covered in scribbled amendments and crossed-out deadlines, and drew a line down the middle of a clean page.

CHICAGO | WILLOW CREEK

She started with Chicago because that's what she knew. That's what made sense.

Creative Director. $$$. Signing bonus $50K - erase personal loan. Clear all debt in six months??

Her pen moved automatically, years of cost-benefit analysis kicking in.

Career advancement. Respect. Validation. Prove Martin wrong. Prove everyone wrong. Corner office. My own team. Real projects. Buildings that matter. Chicago. Culture. Restaurants. Museums. Everything at your fingertips.

The list grew. Each item was true. Each item mattered. She stared at the words and waited to feel the old hunger, the old drive that had carried her through six years of proving herself.

Nothing came. The words sat flat on the page, like a menu from a restaurant she'd once enjoyed but outgrown.

She flipped the pen to the other column.

Willow Creek.

Her hand hesitated over the paper. What did she even write here? The salary was zero. The career prospects were... what? Small-town contractor? That wasn't even a career, it was a hobby. A fantasy. Something city people did when they burned out and needed to "find themselves" before inevitably returning to real life.

She pressed the pen to paper anyway.

Liam.

Just his name. But her chest went tight writing it, and she had to stop and press her palm over her sternum like that might contain the ache blooming there.

God, she was being ridiculous. Making a life decision based on a man she'd known for a few weeks. This was exactly the kind of thing she would have mocked two months ago, some woman throwing away her career for a relationship that probably wouldn't even last a year.

But it wasn't just about Liam. It was...

Mama C's coffee. Mornings that don't start with panic. Work that feels like creation, not performance. Knowing my neighbors. Being known. Mattering to people who see me, not just what I produce. Sawdust and pine. Calluses that mean something. Building things that last.

The pen moved faster now.

Waking up excited instead of dreading the day. Watching the sun rise over mountains. The sound of the creek at night. This house. OUR house. The one we saved together.

She stopped writing and stared at the two columns. Chicago's list was longer, more impressive, full of concrete measurables. Willow Creek's list looked pathetic by comparison—just feelings and intangibles and wishes that couldn't be quantified in a performance review.

But which list made her hands stop shaking?

Ava set down the pen and stood. She couldn't think like this, trapped in the kitchen with Martin's cologne still hanging in the air and Liam's absence screaming from every corner. She needed to move.

She grabbed Beatrice's quilt from the sofa and wrapped it around her shoulders, then walked through the house in the dark, not bothering to turn on lights. Her feet knew the way now, every creaking board, every slightly uneven floorboard they hadn't quite gotten level. In the hallway, she ran her hand along the banister they'd rebuilt together. Solid oak, each baluster hand-turned to match the original specifications. Liam had spent two full days on the lathe getting them perfect, muttering curses when the grain didn't cooperate, starting over when he wasn't satisfied.

"It matters," he'd said when she suggested they could just buy pre-made spindles from the hardware store. "The next person who lives here, they'll touch this railing every day. It should be something worth touching."

The next person who lives here.

The phrase hit her like cold water. She'd been so focused on selling the house that she'd never actually pictured someone else living in it. Someone else making coffee in the kitchen where she and Liam had shared pastries and terrible jokes. Someone else sleeping in the bedroom where they'd torn out mold and built something clean and new. Someone else sitting on the porch swing while watching the sunset paint the mountains purple and gold.

The thought made her physically ill.

Ava sank down onto the stairs, pulling the quilt tighter around herself. Her rational brain was still trying to make the case for Chicago. You're being emotional, you need to think long-term, what about five years from now, ten years from now?

But her hands were gripping the banister like a lifeline, and her chest was tight, her breathing constricted at the very thought of leaving.

When had this happened? When had she stopped thinking of this place as a project and started thinking of it as home?

Her phone buzzed again. She almost ignored it, but muscle memory made her check. Not Martin this time. Maya.

"Are you okay? You've been radio silent for hours. Getting worried" it read.

Ava's fingers trembled as she typed "Martin was here. Offered me Creative Director. Wants an answer tomorrow."

The response came immediately. "WHAT. Creative Director???? Ava that's HUGE."

Three dots appeared, disappeared, appeared again. Then: "Are you taking it?"

Ava stared at the question. This morning, even this afternoon, the answer would have been obvious. Of course she was taking it. Everything she'd worked for, handed to her on a silver platter.

But her fingers typed "I don't know."

"You DON'T KNOW?" A string of shocked emojis followed. "Six years. This is everything you wanted."

"Everything I THOUGHT I wanted," Ava wrote back. Then, before she could second-guess herself, "I'm happy here, Maya. Actually happy. Not pretending-everything's-fine happy. Not I'll-be-happy-once-I-get-the-promotion happy. Just... happy."

The three dots appeared and stayed there for a long time. Finally the message "Are you in love with him?"

Ava closed her eyes. Was she? They'd never said the words. They'd barely kissed. They'd spent weeks arguing about crown molding and sanding floors and learning how to work together. That wasn't love. That was...

"Yes," she typed. "I think I am."

"Then screw the corner office!!!" Maya wrote back immediately. "Come on, Ava. You've been miserable in Chicago for YEARS. I've watched you get smaller and smaller, like that job was shrinking you. And now you're telling me you found something that makes you actually happy, and you're considering giving it up for what? A title? Money?"

"Maya, it's not that simple. I have debt. I have obligations. I can't just leave."

"Yes you can. That's literally what you can do. You can choose yourself. You can choose happy over impressive. When did you become the kind of person who picks the corner office over the guy who makes you laugh?"

The words hit Ava like a slap. When *had* she become that person?

She remembered being twenty-two, fresh out of architecture school, full of dreams about creating beautiful spaces that would make people's lives better. When had that turned into maximizing billable hours and fighting for promotions she didn't even want?

She stood, the quilt falling from her shoulders, and walked to the living room window. Outside, Willow Creek was dark except for scattered porch lights down the road. Small. Quiet. The kind of place she would have dismissed without a second thought two months ago.

But she could picture her life here now with perfect clarity. Mornings with Liam's terrible nuclear coffee and Mama C's pastries. Days spent restoring houses, bringing beauty back to places everyone else had given up on. Evenings on this porch swing, watching the seasons change. Building something that mattered, even if it didn't come with a business card or a LinkedIn update.

She could picture growing old here. And the thought didn't terrify her, instead it gave her joy, like coming home.

Ava turned from the window and looked around the living room. The fireplace they'd cleaned together. The built-in shelves Liam had restored with reverent hands. The floors they'd sanded on their knees, talking about nothing and everything. Every inch of this house held a memory. Every surface was proof that she could create something beautiful with her own hands.

The cottage didn't feel like a project anymore. It felt like hers.

No. Theirs.

Her phone buzzed one more time. Maya: "Whatever you decide, I love you. But babe, I've never heard you sound like yourself until you started talking about this town. Just saying."

Ava's eyes stung. She picked up the quilt and wrapped it around herself again, then walked back to the kitchen. The contract was still there, white and official and promising everything she'd fought for.

She looked at the two columns on her notepad. Chicago's list of impressive achievements. Willow Creek's list of intangibles and feelings.

Which one made her hands stop shaking?

Ava picked up the pen and wrote one more thing under the Willow Creek column, this one in all caps: I GET TO BE MYSELF.

She stared at those words for a long time. Then she flipped the contract over to its blank back page and began to write.

Dear Martin,

Thank you for the offer. I'm honored that you thought of me, and I appreciate you making the trip to Willow Creek.

However, I must decline. Effective immediately, I am resigning from my position. I will not be returning to Chicago.

This is not a negotiation, and it's not a bid for better terms. This is me choosing a different path, one that includes sawdust and small towns and a life that makes me feel like myself instead of like a performance of who I'm supposed to be.

I hope you find someone brilliant for the position. I hope Derek's replacement loves it as much as I once thought I would.

But that person isn't me anymore.

Sincerely, Ava Gardiner

She set down the pen and stared at what she'd written, her heart pounding. Then she flipped the contract over, to the execution section on the front page, and wrote in the signature box. It felt reckless and terrifying and absolutely right.

She was done. Done with corner offices and proving herself and measuring her worth by other people's standards. Done with being the woman who'd forgotten how to want things that couldn't be quantified in a performance review. She was staying. In Willow Creek, in this cottage, in this life that she'd stumbled into and somehow made her own. Now she just had to get Liam back.

A Permanent Foundation

The first hint of dawn was painting the sky in shades of rose and gold when Ava grabbed her keys and made for the door. She wasn't going to the airport. Wasn't going back to Chicago to pack up her old life or say goodbye to the ghost of who she used to be. She was going to Liam's workshop, a converted barn on the edge of his property where he spent his early mornings working on the furniture commissions that were his real passion. She'd find him there, surrounded by wood shavings and the smell of linseed oil, and she'd tell him everything she should have said last night. That she was staying. That she was his, if he still wanted her. That Chicago could keep its corner offices and six-figure salaries, because she'd found something here worth more than all of it combined.

That he was what she burned for.

She climbed into her car, her contract on the seat next to her, ready to drop to Martin at the motel on the edge of town on the way back. She pulled out of the driveway as the sun crept over the mountains.

Willow Creek was beautiful in the early morning light. She drove slowly down Main Street, taking it all in, Mama's Diner where the lights were just flickering on, the hardware store, the post office where Silas would arrive in another hour, the town square where she'd danced with Liam under the stars. This wasn't a backwater town or a temporary stop on her way to somewhere better. This was home. These were her people, the ones who'd watched her struggle and stumble and slowly, impossibly, fall in love with the very thing she'd planned to leave behind.

The community center was already showing signs of life, volunteers gathering for the weekend farmer's market. Mrs Gable waved, coffee cup in hand, and Ava found herself waving back, a genuine smile spreading across her face. She belonged here. Finally, miraculously, she belonged.

Just out the other side of town, Liam's property appeared on her right, the long driveway cutting through a meadow where wildflowers were just beginning to bloom. Ava's heart hammered as she made the turn, already rehearsing what she'd say.

I'm sorry. I was scared. I was angry that you didn't believe you were enough, when you're everything. You're everything, and I'm staying, and please, please don't give up on us.

But when she pulled up to the workshop, her heart sank.

Liam's truck was gone.

Ava sat in her car, staring at the empty space where his truck should have been, where she'd imagined it would be at this hour because Liam was nothing if not predictable in his routines.

The workshop door was closed. The lights were off. Even Barnaby, who usually came running at the sound of any vehicle, was nowhere to be seen.

She was too late.

The thought hit her like a physical blow. While she'd been sitting in her kitchen writing resignation letters and making brave choices, Liam had already left. Maybe he'd gone camping, she thought. Or wandering the woods. Or maybe he'd decided he couldn't stand to be in Willow Creek and packed up and left. Maybe she'd broken something that couldn't be fixed with pretty words and grand gestures.

Ava rested her forehead against the steering wheel, the sunrise she'd found so beautiful moments ago now feeling like a cruel irony. She'd finally figured out what she wanted, finally found the courage to reach for it. And she was too late.

The contract sat on the passenger seat like an accusation.

Ava had been staring at it for the better part of an hour, parked in the gravel lot outside Liam's workshop, her car engine ticking as it cooled in the crisp morning air. Her phone buzzed for the third time. Martin, no doubt, wondering where she was. He had the magnanimous patience of a man who already knew he'd won.

Except he hadn't won. Not even close.

Ava looked down at the contract again, at the heavy cream paper with its embossed letterhead. *Creative Director.* Her own team. Six figures. Everything she'd worked toward for a decade, handed to her on a silver platter.

And she looked at the signature block, where she had written: *I choose different now.*

A fat lot of good that had done for her, sitting in the car for the last hour. She had wanted to confront Martin with Liam at her side. Fate had other ideas.

She was about to give up and head to the motel alone when the knock on her window made her jump so hard she nearly hit her head on the roof.

Liam stood outside her car, one hand raised mid-knock, his expression guarded and exhausted and achingly familiar. He was wearing his work clothes, faded jeans and a blue flannel shirt rolled to his elbows, sawdust clinging to the dark hair on his forearms. He looked like he hadn't slept, dark circles under eyes that tracked to the contract in her lap before meeting her gaze again.

He made that same rolling motion with his hand that he'd made that very first day.

But Ava was already moving, fumbling with the door handle, nearly tripping as she stumbled out of the car. The contract fluttered to the ground between them, her scrawled rejection visible on the signature line.

"I'm not signing it," she said, the words tumbling out before he could speak. "I'm telling Martin no. I'm not leaving Willow Creek."

Liam went very still. "!" he said.

"The house isn't for sale." She was talking too fast, her heart hammering so hard she could feel it in her throat. "I mean, I know we talked about listing it, and the real estate agent has the photos ready, but I can't. I can't sell it, Liam. I can't leave it. I can't..." Her voice cracked. "I can't leave *you*."

Something shifted in his expression, his eyes opened wider and his shoulders relaxed.

"I'm not a closer anymore," Ava continued, her hands twisting together. "I don't want to be the person who packages nice little drawings up and moves on to the next deal. I want to be a builder. I want to create things that last, things that matter. I want..." She took a shaky breath. "I want sawdust in my hair and paint on my jeans and mornings that smell like coffee and pine because you're standing in my kitchen teaching me the proper way to sand a windowsill."

"Ava." Her name came out rough, almost broken.

"I want you there, every day. Not just in the kitchen, in every room, at every minute because...because I'm falling in love with you," she almost shouted it with enthusiasm. "I think I have been since you handed me that pry bar and told me to work. Since you showed me how to read wood grain and listen to what the house was trying to tell us. Since you looked at me covered in plaster dust and made me feel like I was worth something beyond my job title and my bank account."

Her chest was rising and falling rapidly now, as was his. His hands clenched at his sides like he was physically restraining himself.

"I smell sawdust and my whole body reacts," Ava said, a laugh catching in her throat. "Leather and coffee and pine, those are your scents, Liam, and they're everywhere in my house now. In my *home*. And I don't want them to go away. I don't want you to go away. I can't imagine waking up tomorrow and not seeing you, not hearing your voice telling me I'm doing something wrong, not feeling..."

She didn't get to finish.

Liam moved like something had broken loose inside him, closing the distance between them in two long strides. His hands came up to frame her face, calloused palms rough and warm against her cheeks, and then his mouth was on hers and Ava forgot how to breathe.

This wasn't like the almost-kisses they'd shared, the moments interrupted by dogs or phones or her own fears. This was desperate and claiming and so full of relief it made her knees weak. His lips moved against hers with a hunger that matched the ache in her chest, and when she gasped his name, he deepened the kiss, one hand sliding into her hair while the other curved around her waist to pull her flush against him.

She could feel every hard plane of his body against her softer curves, could taste coffee and something sweet on his tongue, could smell sawdust and soap and *him*. Her hands fisted in his shirt, holding on like he might disappear if she let go, and when he tilted her head to change the angle, she made a sound she'd never heard herself make before, needy and wanting and completely unbidden.

"Say it again," he murmured against her mouth, his voice wrecked. "Tell me you're not leaving."

"I'm not leaving," she breathed. "I'm staying. I'm home."

The sound he made was somewhere between a laugh and a groan. He kissed her again, softer this time but no less intense, his thumb stroking along her jaw in a gesture so tender it made her eyes sting.

When they finally broke apart, both breathing hard, Liam pressed his forehead to hers. "I thought I'd lost you," he said roughly. "When you...I thought you'd already decided to go back."

"I was scared," Ava admitted. "Of what choosing you meant. Of what choosing this life meant."

"And now?"

She pulled back just enough to meet his eyes, and saw the vulnerability there that matched her own. "Now I'm more scared of what walking away would mean." She touched his face, tracing the line of his jaw with fingers that trembled slightly. "Take me home, Liam. To our house. The one we built together."

His answer was to kiss her again, quick and hard and full of promise, before threading his fingers through hers and leading her to his truck.

The cottage looked different this morning. Or maybe Ava was different, and that changed how she saw everything else.

Martin hadn't taken the news well, but Ava hadn't given him time to fully react. In a swift movement she'd wanted to do for years, she had tossed the contract on the table in his room, briefly said she wasn't interested, and turned before he could say a word.

It was the second greatest feeling she'd had so far today.

Liam's hand was warm in hers as he led her up the front steps, the same steps he'd repaired that first week, the ones that no longer creaked under their weight. The porch boards were solid beneath her feet, the railing smooth under her palm, everything strong and true and built to last.

He paused at the door, his key already in the lock, and turned to look at her. "You're sure?"

In answer, Ava rose on her toes and kissed him, soft and sweet and certain. "I've never been more sure of anything."

The door swung open on hinges they'd oiled together, revealing the home they'd created. The late morning sun streamed through windows they'd polished, highlighting floors they'd sanded and walls they'd painted. Every surface held a memory, the crown molding he'd taught her to cut, the built-in shelves where they'd argued about historical accuracy, the kitchen where she'd made him coffee every morning.

This wasn't her house anymore. It was theirs.

Liam closed the door behind them and reached for her again, his hands finding her waist with a sureness that made her breath catch. "I've wanted this," he said against her mouth. "Wanted you. For weeks now. But I thought..."

"I know." She kissed him again, deeper this time, her fingers working at the buttons of his flannel. "I thought so too. That you were temporary, that this was temporary, that I'd just go back to who I was before." The shirt fell open, revealing the white t-shirt beneath, and she pressed her palms flat against his chest, feeling the rapid beat of his heart. "But

I don't want to be her anymore. I want to be this version. The one who belongs here. With you."

Something in his expression cracked open, raw and honest. "Ava."

She took his hand and led him toward the stairs, toward the master bedroom where they'd torn out black mold and stripped walls down to the studs. The room where they'd replaced decay with something clean and new, where every surface spoke of second chances and fresh starts. The bed was new, she'd bought it last week, a ridiculous extravagance when she'd still been planning to sell. But she'd wanted something that was *hers*, not inherited, not borrowed.

Liam had helped her bring it up and assemble it with his strong hands. Now those same hands were sliding under her shirt, callused palms rough against the soft skin of her waist, and Ava's breath stuttered in her chest.

"Tell me if I..." he started, but she cut him off with another kiss, her fingers tangling in his hair.

"Don't stop," she whispered against his mouth. "Please, Liam. Don't stop."

He lifted her shirt over her head in one smooth motion, his eyes darkening as they traced over her. She'd never felt more exposed or more seen, standing there in the bedroom they'd rebuilt together while he looked at her like she was something precious he was afraid to break.

"You're so beautiful," he said roughly. "God, Ava, you're so beautiful."

She reached for his shirt, pulled it over his head and let it fall to the floor. His chest was exactly as she'd imagined it, broad and solid, marked with the scars of a life spent working with his hands. There was a thin white line across his ribs where he'd caught himself on a nail, a darker patch on his shoulder from an old burn, and she traced each imperfection with reverent fingers.

"These hands," she murmured, catching one of his and bringing it to her lips. "They saved this house. They taught me how to see beauty in broken things. And they're going to be gentle with me now," she continued, pressing his palm flat against her sternum, over her racing heart. "Aren't they?"

His answer was to lower his mouth to hers again, to walk her backward until her legs hit the edge of the bed. She went willingly, pulling him down with her, and the contrast of their bodies, his solid muscle against her soft curves, sent heat spiraling through her belly.

This was intimacy, she realized. Not just the physical joining that would come, but this, the trust required to be seen completely, to let someone witness your vulnerability and believe they'd honor it. The final inspection of two people who'd stripped away all their protective layers and found something worth keeping underneath.

Liam's mouth traced a path down her throat, across her collarbone, and Ava arched into his touch with a gasp that might have embarrassed her if she'd had the capacity to care. But all she could focus on was the feel of him, the rasp of stubble against sensitive skin, the warmth of his breath, the careful way his hands mapped her body like he was memorizing every curve and hollow.

"I've got you," he murmured against her skin. "I've got you, Ava."

And she believed him.

Later, much later, they lay tangled together in the sheets, the afternoon sun painting golden stripes across the bed through the windows they'd installed side by side. Ava's head was pillowed on Liam's chest, her fingers tracing lazy patterns through the hair there, while his hand stroked up and down her spine in a rhythm that matched his breathing.

Everything was different now. The air seemed clearer, the light brighter, like the world had shifted into sharper focus.

"What are you thinking?" Liam's voice rumbled beneath her ear.

Ava tilted her head to look up at him. His hair was thoroughly messed, her doing, and his lips were slightly swollen from her kisses. He looked rumpled and satisfied and hers, and the fierce possessiveness of that thought made her smile.

"I'm thinking," she said slowly, "that I need to call a real estate agent."

He tensed beneath her. "Ava..."

"Not to sell," she said quickly, pressing a kiss to his chest. "To buy. I want to make an offer on the house next door to Mrs Gable. The blue Victorian that's been on the market for six months."

Liam propped himself up on one elbow to look at her properly. "You want to flip another house?"

"I want to restore it," Ava corrected. "Properly. The way we did this one." She sat up, pulling the sheet around herself, her mind already racing with possibilities. "Mrs Gable says it has original crown molding and pocket doors. The listing says it needs work, but I've learned that 'needs work' just means 'needs someone who cares enough to do it right.' I can write a business case for the bank to convince them to give us finance to fund the operation and we can do the work properly funded by the expected increase in value."

The smile that spread across Liam's face was slow and devastating. "You want to start a restoration business?"

"*We*," Ava corrected. "I want *us* to start a restoration business. I have an eye for design and the business experience. You have the craftsmanship and the knowledge of historical techniques. We can restore this town, piece by piece. We don't have to make a lot of money, we just need to do a good job from project to project and I think we will stay well ahead." She leaned down to kiss him, quick and hard. "We make a good team, McGregor."

"The best," he agreed, pulling her back down against his chest. "Though we might need to establish some ground rules about workplace conduct."

Ava laughed, the sound bright and unguarded. "Absolutely. Very professional. No kissing in the kitchen."

"Or the hallway."

"Or the bedroom while we're working on crown molding."

"That's going to be difficult," Liam murmured against her hair. "You're very distracting when you're wearing a tool belt."

She was about to respond when her phone buzzed from somewhere on the floor. They both ignored it, but it buzzed again. And again.

With a sigh, Ava extracted herself from Liam's arms and padded across the room to fish the phone out of her jeans pocket. The screen showed a string of increasingly frantic texts from Maya:

"ANSWER YOUR PHONE"

"Did you sign????"

"Ava I swear to god if you ghosted me to spiral alone"

Ava smiled and typed back: "I'm home."

The response was immediate: "what does that mean??"

"Exactly what it sounds like. I'm staying. In Willow Creek. Forever."

Her phone immediately started ringing. Ava answered on speaker, climbing back into bed and tucking herself against Liam's side.

"WHAT?" Maya's shriek was loud enough to make them both wince. "You're staying? You turned down Creative Director? Are you insane?"

"Probably," Ava admitted cheerfully.

"Is he there? Is Hottie Contractor there right now?"

Liam's laugh was a low rumble. "Hi, Maya."

"Oh my god, he IS there. At—" there was a pause, presumably while Maya checked the time "—two in the afternoon on a Wednesday. Ava Gardiner, did you finally—"

"Goodbye, Maya," Ava said, her face burning.

"WAIT. I need details. I need—"

Ava hung up, tossing the phone aside. "She's going to call back."

"Undoubtedly." Liam pulled her closer, pressing a kiss to her temple. "Your mother's next."

"Tomorrow's problem," Ava decided. "Today, I just want to be here. With you. In our house."

Our house. The words settled into her chest with a rightness that defied logic. A month ago, she'd been a different person, driven and ambitious and absolutely certain of who she was and what she wanted. A month ago, this life would have looked like failure, like settling, like giving up on everything she'd worked for.

Now it looked like coming home.

Ava woke to sunlight streaming through the windows they'd polished together, warm and golden against her bare skin. For a moment, she lay still, letting herself adjust to the unfamiliar sensation of waking up next to someone, of feeling the solid weight of Liam's arm across her waist and the slow rise and fall of his breathing against her back.

This was real. This was happening.

This was *hers*.

Her phone buzzed on the nightstand, and she reached for it carefully, trying not to wake Liam. The screen showed a message from Maya, sent at some ungodly hour: "I can't sleep. You broke my brain. Call me when you're vertical again."

Ava smiled and typed back: "I'm home."

The response came immediately, like Maya had been waiting: "I KNOW THAT ALREADY. But... are you happy?"

Ava looked around the room they'd finished together, the soft cream walls they'd painted, the refinished floors that glowed in the morning light, the windows that now opened smoothly after Liam had spent an entire afternoon repairing the old sash weights. She thought about the kitchen downstairs where they'd argued over cabinet placement, the hall where they'd shared their first almost-kiss, the bathroom where she'd learned how to properly grout tile. Every inch of this house held a memory. Every surface spoke of something they'd built together, of patience and care and choosing to honor what came before while creating something new.

Liam shifted behind her, his arm tightening around her waist as he pressed a sleepy kiss to her shoulder. "Morning," he mumbled against her skin.

"Morning," she whispered back.

Her fingers hovered over her phone's keyboard for a moment, then typed: "I'm home. And yes. I'm happy."

Maya's response was a string of heart emojis followed by: "Good. You deserve it. Both of you."

Ava set the phone aside and turned in Liam's arms, finding him watching her with sleepy eyes and a soft smile that made her heart squeeze.

"No regrets?" he asked quietly.

She thought about Martin and his contract, about the corner office she'd coveted, about the life she'd built in Chicago that had looked so perfect from the outside while slowly hollowing her out from within. She thought about power lunches and board meetings and the constant pressure to prove herself worthy of space in rooms that didn't want her there. She thought about the balloon payment she will almost certainly miss and the consequences she'd have to face in the next couple of weeks unless she came up with a new plan.

Then she looked at the man beside her, the one who'd handed her a pry bar and taught her the difference between tearing down and building up. The one who'd seen her covered in plaster dust and paint and treated her like she was the most capable person he'd ever met. The one who'd made her believe that home wasn't a place you escaped from, but a place you built with your own hands and filled with people worth keeping.

"No regrets," she said firmly. "Not a single one."

Liam's smile widened, and he pulled her closer, tucking her head beneath his chin. They lay like that as the sun climbed higher, warming the room they'd saved from decay. Ava exhaled and let go of years of accumulated fears and doubts, knowing she was exactly where she was supposed to be.

For the first time in her life, Ava Gardiner wasn't running toward something or away from something else. She wasn't performing or proving or pretending. She was just... home. And that was more than enough.

Outside, Willow Creek was waking up. Mrs Gable was probably already at her window, binoculars at the ready. Silas would be making his morning rounds, spreading news faster than the internet ever could.

Mama C would be at the diner, preparing her daily specials and telling anyone who'd listen that she'd known all along how this would end.

The cottage, Beatrice's cottage, Ava's cottage, their cottage, stood solid and strong on its foundation, its windows gleaming in the morning sun, its heart beating steady and true. Ready for whatever came next.

The Final Inspection

The construction sign was gone.

Ava stood at the edge of the driveway, coffee mug in her hand in the cool morning air, and stared back at the little cottage that she'd first set eyes on almost two months ago. It had been a renovation that completely changed her life, and like her the little house had been holding its breath the whole time, and could finally exhale.

The cottage didn't look like it was holding anything back now. Once she quit Chicago and gave herself the time the house really needed, she and Liam had achieved something they could be very proud of. It practically glowed in the late autumn sunlight, the fresh cream paint on the trim gleaming against the restored yellow siding. The porch no longer sagged like a tired sigh but stood straight and proud, its new railings sturdy beneath her touch when she'd tested them this morning. The windows caught the light and threw it back in clean, honest reflections, no longer obscured by decades of grime and neglect.

It was finished.

The thought should have filled her with relief, with triumph, with the satisfaction of a project now complete. Instead, she was filled with wonder, tinged with an ache she couldn't quite name.

Her phone pinged. She glanced at it, and smiled.

"You're going to freeze out here." Liam's voice came from the house, accompanied by the creak of the screen door, the one he'd rehung last week with the original brass hinges they'd found under the house. His footsteps crossed the porch, solid and sure on the boards they'd sanded together, and he strolled up to be with her.

Ava smiled as his arms came around her from behind, his chest warm against her back. "I'm looking at it."

"I can see that." His chin settled on top of her head, and they stood like that for a moment, both of them taking in what they'd built. "Still can't believe it's done."

"Done-ish," Ava corrected, leaning back into his warmth. "We still need to hang that photo of Beatrice in the hallway."

"Done-ish," Liam agreed, the smile in his voice evident. "Though knowing you, you'll find seventeen other things that need tweaking before the open house this afternoon."

He wasn't wrong. Even now, her architect's eye was cataloging details, the way the morning light hit the kitchen window at just the right angle, how the garden path they'd rebuilt seemed to draw the eye naturally toward the front door, the perfect proportions of the porch columns they'd restored to their original Victorian specifications. But she wasn't critiquing anymore. She was appreciating. Savoring. Memorizing every detail of this place that had somehow become the most important project of her life.

"News?" Liam asked, of the phone in her hand.

"The settlement completed overnight. My cupboard that I called a studio apartment is no longer my concern."

"Hooray, we should celebrate. You happy?"

She nodded slowly and deeply. Words wouldn't come close to capturing her feelings. "I arrived in Willow Creek with dreams of coming out debt free and trading up back in Chicago. It certainly hasn't panned out that way." Funny how life never seems to pan out the way you think it will, she thought with a smile. "But I'm walking away with enough to clear that damn personal loan and that's the main thing. And while I may not be debt free, I'm trading way, way up." She reached up and gave him a kiss.

"So yes?"

"Yes!" she giggled.

"Come on then," he said, pressing an extra kiss to the top of her head. "That photo won't hang itself."

The hardwood floors practically sparkled beneath their feet as they walked through the house. Oak once buried under linoleum and carpet, now restored to its original honey-gold glory. Ava ran her hand along the staircase railing as she passed, feeling the smooth wood beneath her palm, remembering the day they'd nearly brought the whole second floor down before shoring up the failing beam. The staircase bannister that had almost killed them, stood solid and secure, its balusters straight and true, the newel post anchored so firmly that Liam had joked they could hang a swing from it.

In the kitchen, the morning light streamed through windows that actually opened and closed, washing over countertops they'd installed together and the vintage stove they'd spent a week tracking down. The room smelled of fresh coffee and possibility. Nothing like the musty decay that had greeted her that first morning.

"Where do you think?" Liam held up the framed photograph of Beatrice, the one they'd found in the attic last week. In it, she stood on the very porch they'd just crossed, maybe fifty or sixty years ago, laughing at something beyond the camera's frame. Her eyes were bright with joy, her whole face lit up with the kind of happiness that couldn't be faked.

Ava studied the hallway, considering placement with the careful eye she'd once reserved for million-dollar developments. But this mattered more than any of those projects ever had. This was personal. This was a legacy. "There," she said, pointing to a spot near the base of the stairs. "So she can watch everyone come and go. She'd like that, I think. Being part of the daily life of the house."

Liam's smile was soft as he moved to the spot she'd indicated. "Yeah. She would."

They hung the picture together, Liam holding the frame while Ava checked the level, both of them making micro-adjustments until it was perfect. Not corporate presentation perfect, but *right* in a way that had nothing to do with straight lines and everything to do with feeling. When they stepped back to admire their work, Beatrice seemed to smile at them from the wall, as if approving of what they'd done with her home.

"We made a good team," Liam said quietly.

"We did." Ava slipped her hand into his, feeling the familiar calluses on his palm, the strength in his fingers as they intertwined with hers. "We do."

He turned to give her a kiss, that despite its brevity still made her legs quiver. He looked intently into her eyes and the expression on his face made her chest tight with emotions she was still learning to name. Not just love, though God yes, that too, but respect. Partnership. The bone-deep certainty that they were equals in this, in everything.

"I talked to Alice Harper yesterday," Liam said, his thumb tracing circles on the back of her hand. "About that old Victorian next to Mrs Gable."

Ava's heart kicked. They'd looked at it last week, both of them admiring the beautiful bones beneath the peeling paint and sagging porch. It needed everything, structural work, electrical updates, probably a new roof. It needed exactly the kind of careful, loving restoration they'd given this cottage.

"And?" She tried to keep her voice steady, professional, but hope leaked through anyway.

"She's interested in our pitch. Full historical restoration, preserving the original details, the works." Liam's smile was tentative, vulnerable in a way that still surprised her. "Wants to meet next week to discuss terms. For McGregor & Gardiner Restoration."

"I thought it was Gardiner & McGregor Restoration?" she teased.

"Details, details," he laughed.

"Next week," Ava repeated, testing the words. A few weeks ago, the concept of "next week" in Willow Creek had been impossible. Now it was inevitable, like gravity or sunrise or the way her hand fit perfectly in Liam's.

"If you want to," Liam added quickly. "I know it's fast, and if you need more time to..."

Ava kissed him, cutting off his nervous rambling with her mouth on his. He made a surprised sound that turned into a hum of pleasure, his free hand coming up to cup her face as he kissed her back with the kind of focused intensity he brought to everything he cared about.

When they finally pulled apart, both slightly breathless, Ava kept her forehead pressed to his. "Yes. To our restoration business. Our partnership. Our future. And yes to the Victorian house. To all of it, yes."

His answering grin was bright enough to light the whole house.

By three o'clock, the cottage was filled with people.

Mama C had taken over the kitchen, directing a small army of helpers as they set out enough food to feed an army. Casserole dishes covered every available surface, alongside pies and cakes and cookies that filled the house with the scent of butter and sugar and home.

Silas held court in the living room, regaling anyone who would listen with stories of the house's history and Beatrice's younger days, his weathered hands gesturing broadly as he described the time she'd chased off a black bear with nothing but a broom and pure determination.

Even Mrs Gable had to grudgingly admit that "the place looks nearly as good as when Beatrice was a girl." Coming from Mrs Gable, it was practically a declaration of love.

Ava moved through the rooms, accepting congratulations and answering questions about the renovation, but she felt oddly detached from the praise. These people weren't complimenting her business acumen or her project management skills. They were thanking her for bringing back something they'd thought was lost. For caring enough to do it right.

"You did good, honey." Mama C appeared at her elbow, pressing a glass of sweet tea into her hand. "Real good."

"We did good," Ava corrected, gesturing to include Liam, who was currently explaining the structural reinforcements to a fascinated cluster of local contractors.

"Mmm hmm" Mama C's eyes sparkled with knowing amusement. "You planning to stick around a long time then? Make an honest man of this boy?"

Heat flooded Ava's cheeks. "Mama C!"

"Because if you are, I should probably tell you that I know for a fact his grandmother's engagement ring is in the safety deposit box at the bank. Been sitting there for years, waiting for the right woman." She patted Ava's hand. "Just something to keep in mind."

She swept away before Ava could formulate a response, leaving her standing in the middle of the living room with her face on fire and her heart doing complicated acrobatics in her chest. Marriage. The thought should have terrified her, it had terrified her two months ago, but so did the thought of spending more than a few weeks in this town. But standing here in this house they'd rebuilt together, surrounded by a community that had become her family, the concept didn't feel like a trap, but rather like a dream come true.

"You okay?" Liam materialized beside her, concern creasing his brow. "You look flushed."

"Mama C just ambushed me with talk of engagement rings."

His eyes went wide, then soft, and the smile that spread across his face was tender enough to make her knees weak. "Did she now?"

"Mm-hmm. Apparently there's one waiting at the bank."

"So I understand," he agreed, not quite meeting her eyes.

They stood there for a moment, the party swirling around them, not saying all the things that hummed in the air between them. Too soon, Ava's rational brain insisted. You've only known him for two months. This is crazy.

But her traitorous, hopeful heart whispered that sometimes crazy was just another word for right.

"Ava?" Silas's voice cut through the moment. "Got a minute?"

She squeezed Liam's hand once before moving to where Silas stood near the hallway, his expression uncharacteristically serious.

"There's something I want to show you," he said quietly. "Been meaning to, but the timing never seemed right."

He led her through the kitchen, towards the pantry they'd so carefully restored, the only quiet place in the house.

"Silas, if you're about to show me another structural issue..."

"No, no, no issues." His smile was gentle as he flipped on the light. "Just history." In his hand he held a letter. "Beatrice was always one for stories and secrets. This one, she left in my care until...well, until now, I reckon."

He handed over the letter with a warm smile, like a kindly grandfather to his favourite grandchild. "She would have been so proud of you," he said. "Well done."

Ava's hands trembled as she opened the missal from her great aunt.

My dearest Ava,

I'm writing this at 86, with arthritic hands and the certain knowledge that my time here is drawing to a close.

I've lived a good life. A rewarding life. Happy with the decisions I made. It may not have been traditional, but I made a home in this house and in this town that was my own, living as who I wanted to be, and I couldn't be happier.

I adored watching you grow up in those summers we had when you were young. I could tell even from the age of 4 what a sparkle you had and would bring to the world. But as you got older, and as you've bloomed into a beautiful young woman, I saw you stalling in that city and not being who you really are. I know what the feeling of being trapped is like, and how difficult it can be to go against expectation. So I gave you this house to give you a chance to be free.

If you are the girl I know, you're reading this now because you made the decision to release that sparkle and choose love over obligation. You've done the work. And I'm so proud of you. You've sanded floors and re-

paired windows and fought with the plumbing. You've cursed my name and maybe even cried in frustration. But you've also fallen in love with this place, haven't you? I can tell because you've made it this far.

This house has a way of claiming people. This town has a way of claiming people. Thirty days was all I thought it would take. I hope I was right!

Thank you for seeing what it could be. Thank you for caring enough to bring it back to life. But thank you, most of all, for being honest to yourself and choosing to be the Ava I know you can be.

This house deserves to be filled with laughter and arguments and all the beautiful chaos of a life fully lived. Make it yours. Make it home.

With all my love, Beatrice

Ava's vision blurred with tears. Silas's weathered hand touched her on her shoulder, steady and warm.

"She knew," Ava whispered. "Somehow, she knew. Me."

"Beatrice always did have a gift for seeing what folks needed before they knew it themselves," Silas said softly. "Reckon she saw what you needed most, a place to belong. A reason to put down roots."

Around them, the party continued, laughter and conversation and the warm buzz of community. Ava clutched Beatrice's letter to her chest.

This was where she belonged.

The party wound down as the sun began its descent toward the mountains, painting the sky in those shades of amber and rose Ava adored. Guests trickled away with hugs and promises to see each other soon until, finally, it was just Ava and Liam, standing on the porch in the evening light.

"Come here," Liam said, tugging her toward the porch swing, the one they'd spent three days fixing, replacing the rusted chains with new hardware that would last another hundred years. They settled together, Ava tucked against Liam's side, his arm warm around her shoulders.

The swing creaked gently as they rocked, a sound that would forever remind her of this moment, this perfect sense of completion.

"Do you miss it?" Liam asked after a while, his voice quiet in the twilight. "The high-rise office? The fancy title?"

Ava looked out at the mountains, purple shadows deepening as the sun sank lower. She thought about her old life and the version of herself she'd built so carefully to survive in that world. That woman was a stranger now. Someone she'd known once but had outgrown, like a childhood friend you remembered fondly but had nothing left to say to.

"You know what?" she said, tilting her head to look up at him. "I think I'm overqualified for that life now."

Liam's laugh was warm and genuine, the sound of it rumbling through his chest against her shoulder. "Overqualified?"

"Mm-hmm. Turns out it takes a lot more skill to save a hundred-year-old house than to flip a property for profit. More courage too." She reached up to trace the line of his jaw, feeling the rasp of evening stubble beneath her fingers. "And I've got a business partner who keeps me honest."

"Is that what I do?" His hand came up to cover hers, pressing her palm against his face.

"Among other things." She stretched up to kiss him, soft and slow and sweet. When she pulled back, she saw her own contentment reflected in his eyes. "Ask me again in a year. When we've finished that Victorian next to Mrs Gable, and taken on whatever other impossible projects this town throws at us."

"And if I ask you something else in a year?" His voice had gone serious, tender in a way that made her heart stutter. "Something that starts with 'Will you' and ends with, I don't know...'marry me'?"

Ava's breath caught. They hadn't talked about this explicitly, not the way Mama C had ambushed her with talk of rings. But sitting here on this porch swing, in front of a house they'd brought back to life with their own hands, the future was suddenly incredibly clear.

"Ask me," she whispered.

"Not yet." Liam pressed a kiss to her forehead, achingly gentle. "Not until we've finished at least one more project together. I want to be sure you know what you're signing up for. A lifetime of stubborn opinions about crown molding and arguments over paint colors."

"Sounds perfect," Ava said, and meant it with her whole heart.

They sat in comfortable silence as the first fireflies began to emerge, tiny sparks of light dancing in the gathering dusk. Behind them, through the open windows, the house glowed warm and welcoming. Lights on in the kitchen, the living room, the upstairs bedroom that had become theirs without either of them quite deciding when. This was what Beatrice had wanted, Ava realized. Not just a restored house, but a living one. A home filled with love and laughter and the beautiful chaos of people building a life together.

"Thank you," she said suddenly.

"For what?"

"For seeing me. The real me, under all that corporate armor." She laced her fingers through his. "For teaching me the difference between flipping and restoring. For showing me that putting down roots isn't the same as being trapped."

Liam's arm tightened around her shoulders. "Thank you for staying. For choosing this." He gestured at the house, the town beyond, the mountains silhouetted against the darkening sky. "For choosing me. Us."

Us. Not just Ava and Liam, but Ava and Willow Creek. Ava and Mama C and Silas. The found family she hadn't known she needed until she had it.

The swing creaked gently as they rocked, and somewhere in the distance, Ava heard laughter, probably teenagers heading to the creek, making memories of their own.

"I love you," Ava said into the comfortable silence. Not because the moment demanded it, but because it was true, and she was done hiding true things.

Liam's smile was soft in the twilight. "I love you too."

They stayed there until the stars came out, wrapped in each other and the thought of a million tomorrows. Two people who'd found each other while finding themselves, who'd learned that sometimes the best things in life weren't the ones you planned for, but the ones you built together, board by board, nail by nail, choice by choice.

The house stood behind them, solid and sure and full of light.

Finally, truly, *home.*

LOVE UNDER RENOVATION